Dave Brown is ne.. .. ..
has been in retail management nearly all his
working life. After suffering a setback in his
health at the age of 58 he retired from work
and took up writing as a pastime. He enjoys
travelling and has visited all five continents.
He now lives in Essex where he engrosses
himself in his writing.

ONE RULE FOR THE BIG CROOKS

Something to read in your retirement

[signature]

ONE RULE FOR THE BIG CROOKS

by

DAVE BROWN

HAMILTON & Co. Publishers
LONDON

Paperback ISBN 1 901668 11 8

Publisher

HAMILTON & Co. Publishers
10 Stratton Street
Mayfair
LONDON

Through life, one makes many acquaintances, but very few friends, the people one encounters every day, one has to learn to tolerate.

Chapter 1.

They met on one of Johnny's afternoon outings to the West End of England's capital, London. Johnny loved the big city, especially the West End, he was fascinated by the hustle and bustle of it all, he enjoyed the lights, the smell and the whole caboodle of Theatreland. He could just be present in the busy atmosphere of the great city, to enjoy the ambience and the charm that strangely for some people the city gave. Hours would pass in no time just browsing in one of the most prestigious shopping areas of the country.

He had just returned to England and was taking a well earned break from his occupation of installation engineer. He was employed by an international company, selling and installing multiple-head, computer-controlled, profile gas-cutting machines. He had been home two days and was taking what he had promised himself whilst working in the heat of Israel for the last three months, a trip to the big city, to see the lights and soak up the atmosphere. His home was at Pitsea, a suburb of Basildon New Town, on the north side of the Thames, about thirty-five miles from London. As with all new towns, they didn't have the character of the big established cities in Johnny's mind. He lodged with his elder brother and his wife and two children at Pitsea. They were pleased to have him, mainly because his job kept him away for long periods at a time, leaving them on their own, in their own little family group and because the rent helped them in their struggle to maintain a decent standard of living and to keep the mortgage payments up-to-date.

Johnny was an extremely good looking young man. He had no family except his elder brother, his parents having both died, they had been married late in life and started their family when most other couples would have thought it too old to start a family. Johnny had put an awful lot of effort into learning engineering, as his school days had not been very successful. The time he spent at school had been more or less wasted, he hadn't been a conscientious scholar; he had spent many of his school days playing truant and doing his best to escape any hard work. His idea of school was to do as little as possible and to make sure that every day was for fun and fun only. As a result, he was at one time put into a remedial stream for backward children because he got so far behind with his lessons. He didn't like school, but when his school days were over he realised what a big mistake he had made and that he should have put the effort in when he had had the chance. Finally realising that the world didn't owe him a living, he joined night school to catch up on his education and during the day he attended engineering college on day release from his employers, where he studied hard and achieved quite a bit of success. He eventually passed his exams and was awarded City and Guild certificates in engineering, which boosted his confidence and made life feel a bit more successful for him. His newly found self esteem made him feel that he wasn't wasting his life and gave him the will to succeed. He was just under six feet tall, his hair was dark; but even at his young age, grey hair was becoming prominent, which gave him an air of distinction which he really didn't deserve, but it did give him the appearance of someone in authority, which went along with his very quick wit.

He had travelled up to London by train and had hailed a black cab as he came out of the railway terminal at Fenchurch Street. The cabby turned the meter down and, pulling away, looked in the rear view mirror and said,

"Where to, Guv?"

"West End, please."

"Right, Guv, whereabouts?"

"Don't matter, anywhere, I've got nothing planned."

The cabby would have liked a little more preciseness, but was quite content to head in the general direction of Theatreland. He had received that sort of request on many an occasion from customers who didn't know London particularly well, and were content to sit back and look at London from the rear seat of a cab, and so he, always on the lookout for extra cash started up a conversation.

"Whaddaya gonna do up West, see a show, Guv?"

"Might do, I'm just going to have a look around and play it by ear."

After a couple of minutes silence, the cabby started up again.

"Not looking for any female company are ya?" he asked looking in the rear view mirror and smiling, his large yellow teeth being one of his most predominant features. Johnny answered the reflection in the driving mirror.

"No, not at the moment," smiling back. "I'm just going to have a look around, maybe a meal or something, and no doubt a couple of beers, then I'll see what happens."

The cabby went quiet, no more chatter when he realised that no extras were going to be required on this trip, and therefore, no bonus, and was content to hum the chorus of Memories, from Cats as he drove through the busy streets of the City of London. This was one of the tunes that Johnny recognised amongst the vague, deep humming tones that were coming from the front of the cab.

After travelling for about a quarter of an hour through the busy London traffic, with Johnny just gazing out of the cab windows, the cabby startled Johnny with,

"This do ya, Guv?" They were entering Regent Street, from the Oxford Street end. The cabby could have stopped earlier, but was waiting for a signal from his fare, forgetting that his customer obviously wasn't too familiar with the big city.

"Yes fine, thanks," Johnny paid the cabby. As he alighted he gave him what he thought was a fair sized tip, thinking the cabby would say something to show his appreciation.

Instead he took the money with, "Thanks, Guv," and he quickly disappeared into the stream of busy traffic that was heading towards Piccadilly Circus.

Johnny stepped back away from the kerb, the mid afternoon sun was warm on the back of his head, as he thought to himself, 'Which way do I go now?' He turned towards Oxford Street, the exhaust fumes from the traffic were quite strong; he had been used to much cleaner air for the last few months whilst working overseas, but he was pleased to be here. He hadn't got any real plans and just dawdled along Regent Street, looking in the windows of the stores and particularly the windows of Liberty's, the famous departmental store. As he walked slowly he noticed two young ladies, giggling and trying to dress a mannequin in a beautiful, gold, full length evening gown. He stood and watched as they made the model look most unsightly, tipping it first one way then the other, and finally laying it down and making it look most undignified, as one of them sat astride it. Johnny stood watching and smiling to himself. The girls knew he was there and made a few uncomplimentary gestures to the half-dressed dummy, then looked in Johnny's direction for approval. He wondered how these two girls could have the talent to make these windows so beautiful, the only tools he could see was a little box of various pliers, tack hammers and packets of pins and the like. He stood and was entertained for many minutes, the two girls sneakily watching him without letting him see that they were looking. The youngest of the two girls, to Johnny, was extremely attractive. She was about twenty-two or twenty-three, short, swept back hair, deep brown in colour, and her complexion, under the lights of the window, was soft, white and blemish free. He tried to catch her eye several times. This she knew, but carried on working as though he wasn't there. Short of banging on the window there wasn't much he could do. The thought of tapping on the window did occur to him, but in front of dozens of people walking by, he hadn't got the nerve. Even if she looked in his direction he would not have been able to

4

make her hear. He gave up, after making sure he could not attract the attention of the two girls. He decided to walk up to Oxford Street and have a wander around the main stores, looking back at the window that had just amused him, for some sign of the young lady that a few minutes before had caught his eye.

He wasn't short of money and he certainly wasn't short of clothes, and he thought to himself, 'What am I doing window shopping?' The size of the stores and the professional way that they were set out fascinated him, and he just dawdled from store to store, taking in the atmosphere. As the afternoon passed and he was tiring of wandering aimlessly around the stores of Oxford Street, he headed back towards Liberty's, hoping to see the two girls again, still working in the windows. To his disappointment the window was finished and there wasn't a sign of the girls to be seen. It was very reassuring to see that the mannequin had regained her modesty, and the rest of the window, though pretty sparse, was beautifully dressed. He was about to continue his walk in the direction of Piccadilly when a voice said,

"Hello! What, have you come back to see her fully dressed?"

He turned, and to his amazement it was the girl he had seen earlier in the window. He didn't know quite how to answer. Her astonishingly good looks took him completely by surprise, but he said without thinking, "No, I came back to see you." Having said it, much to his own surprise, he waited for an answer. Thinking to himself, 'I've pushed my luck here,' and hoping it didn't show, he could feel his face starting to colour up with a bit of embarrassment.

"Oh, I thought you had come back to inspect my work," she said. He could see that she was also slightly embarrassed. He could also see that she was not in her working clothes, she was dressed in a very smart two-piece suit, beige in colour and it fitted her perfectly and showed off her extremely shapely figure. She wore a soft tangerine scarf around her neck which matched her shoes and handbag, and the blouse she wore was the same colour as her hair, a deep, rich brown. It was obvious that she had a flare for colour co-ordination and that as a window dresser, she must have had a feel for anything artistic.

"I always go round and check my windows every evening before going home, just to make sure that I haven't forgotten anything," she said, trying to keep the conversation going.

"Does that mean you are finished for the day, then?"

"Yes, I'm off home now," she answered, feeling that Johnny was going to pursue the conversation.

"Where's home?"

"What do you want to know for? I have to catch a train," she answered hesitantly.

"So do I, I live at Pitsea in Essex."

She smiled, and looked at Johnny in disbelief.

"Do you now, well there's a coincidence, I live at Vange, so I have to go to Pitsea station."

"That's nice, so you will be wanting some company to travel home with then?"

"I don't know, I don't usually allow myself to be picked up on the street."

"Picked up on the street?" Johnny smiled. "We have known each other all the afternoon," and continued, "we're going the same way, anyway, so what's the harm?"

"I'm not sure, nothing, I suppose."

"Well, come on then."

"Oh! All right then, I don't suppose there is any thing wrong with it."

"Good! What's your name? What shall I call you?"

"My name is Susan, but my friends call me Sue."

"Right then, Sue, let's go. My name's Johnny."

They started off towards Oxford Street with a view to catching the underground. They were both chatting away as if they had known each other for years, full of excitement. Johnny couldn't believe his luck, he was delighted to be in the company of such a beautiful woman and she had similar thoughts about Johnny. They were oblivious to the people

6

that were around them and, although the train was packed with rush hour commuters, they didn't see anyone else in the carriage with them, they had eyes only for each other. The journey which seemed very short was over in no time, much to the disappointment of both of them.

When the train reached Pitsea, the two of them walked the mile or so to Vange. Johnny didn't want to leave her, they seemed to have so much in common, and arrangements were made to meet each other for a meal later in the evening at the Five Bells public house at Vange, reasonably near to where both of them lived.

The two parted, both very excited and each went home to smarten themselves up to be together later in the evening. Johnny was especially excited at the idea of a date with such a lovely girl. As he made his way to his brother's house, he thought to himself, 'Of all the girls I've met, I think this is the one for me,' and his step lengthened and he whistled as he thought over what had happened to him that day. 'I wish that I had given that cabby a larger tip for dropping me just where he did,' he thought to himself, 'and to think I told him I wasn't interested in female company.' He smiled and increased his speed a little more so as to give himself plenty of time to really spruce himself up for his evening date.

Chapter 2.

He got to the public house about an hour before the time that they had agreed to meet. The Five Bells pub was a very busy place, situated on a major cross-roads, and was recognised locally as an eating place to celebrate all sorts of special occasions, and indeed this evening was no exception. Several groups were already eating and, more than once, 'Happy Birthday' could be heard being sung, coming from the direction of the main eating area. Johnny sat in one of the bay windows of the bar while he waited, so that he might catch a glimpse of Sue as she approached the inn. He had first one pint and then another, the beer was going down extremely easily, maybe it was nerves, it was definitely excitement. The light outside was beginning to fail. He had his third pint and was beginning to get agitated. He kept looking at his watch, she was late. 'One more pint, then she will be here,' he thought as he looked up the road in the direction of her house. He didn't know exactly where she lived, only the approximate area. He was slowly getting drunk and was cursing to himself inside. 'She had no intentions of turning up,' he thought and was getting annoyed and irritable. The beer wasn't helping and he started to chat to a couple of fellows that had booked a table for a meal. He was pretty much worse the wear for drink, wasn't making much sense with his conversation and they soon began to ignore him. Johnny checked the time again, she was now nearly two hours late. 'The bitch,' he thought, 'she had no intentions of turning up. One more, then if she isn't here I'm going,' he said to himself. He still sat, looking out of the window, although it was dark outside now. This was Johnny's signal to give up and make his way home. He left the pub feeling disappointed and dejected, he had sat and waited for a woman for almost three hours.

"Must be going soft in the head," he shouted out loud to himself in his inebriated state, but he couldn't help feeling utterly disappointed and let down. 'Who needs bloody women anyway,' he thought as he headed home. His route home took him past the area where Sue lived. It's a good job he never knew exactly where she lived, or he might have made himself look very foolish.

Next morning, he had got the house to himself. He woke late and didn't feel exactly on top of the world, his head felt a bit heavy from the night before. His brother and wife were both at work and the two children were at school. The extra lay in bed hadn't helped the way he felt, the air of disappointment was still about him and the previous night's beer had clouded his brain. He sat and tried to work out where he had gone wrong the night before. Over a strong coffee, he came to the conclusion that he had not put a foot wrong. He had done as he promised, she must have misunderstood the meeting place. The more he thought about it the more he came to the conclusion that she deserved another chance. He became more excited, he washed, shaved and dressed, and prepared himself for a second encounter with the lovely Susan and set off for Regent Street, for the second time in that week.

Arriving at Regent Street once again, he stood for several minutes looking in the windows of the famous departmental store. First one window, then the next, all the way along the street. To his disappointment, there wasn't anybody working in the windows. All the windows were fully dressed and he found them very interesting with many different themes, all beautifully displayed, but he hadn't come to admire the windows, he was there to find out why he had been stood up the night before. The main entrance of the big store was manned by a commissionaire in uniform, a tall man, very stern looking, in a purple suit with tails and a top hat, immaculately turned out. Johnny thought of asking him how to contact the window dressers, but changed his mind. The uniform put him off. He thought the man looked far too superior to answer such a question. He went inside and wandered around the store, hoping to catch a glimpse of Susan. Surprisingly, there weren't many people inside.

He wondered how an enormous store of that size, in that very exclusive part of London, could possibly make a profit with so few customers. He looked in most of the internal sections of the departmental store for some sign of Sue, with no luck. Eventually, his attention was drawn to a small tool- box laying open on one of the fixtures in the menswear department, very similar to the one he had seen in the window the day before. He drew a little nearer to see if he could see inside the small box. He noticed inside that there were pins, and staples, and the same type of tools he had seen in the box in the window yesterday. 'It must be hers,' he thought, 'there can't be many boxes like that, unless it is an issued item from the firm. Right,' he thought, 'I'll hang around and see who it belongs to, someone must be using it and I'm going to hang around and see who it is.' He didn't have to wait too long, soon a woman of middle age arrived, quite small in stature and dressed in a brown smock, and proceeded to dress the fixture with brightly coloured paper. It was obviously going to be a display for gentlemen's trousers.

Johnny plucked up courage. Approaching the woman he said,

"Excuse me, do you know how I can contact Susan?" The lady, was very surprised that anyone dared to speak to her while she was working.

Glaring down her nose at the embarrassed Johnny she said, "Susan! Susan who?" She looked Johnny up and down and stood waiting for a reply in a very superior manner, which was really only an act, not many people spoke to her whilst she was working and when they did, she liked to show how important she was.

"I'm sorry, but I don't know her surname, but she does work here as a window dresser."

The woman looked harshly at Johnny, she could see that he was embarrassed, she felt a bit sorry for him which made her relax her attitude. After waiting for a short time just to let Johnny know that she was doing him a favour, she answered. "Oh, Sue! You mean Sue, she's printing tickets in the printing room. Would you like me to fetch her for you," and without waiting for an answer she put down the pliers she was holding and closed the small toolbox. "Who shall I say wants her?"

"Tell her it's Johnny and that I'm having a coffee in the restaurant, thank you." He felt apprehensive and grateful, he had no idea what to expect when he saw Sue again.

The woman hastened away and, as she went, looked back at Johnny a couple of times over her shoulder, as if to make sure she wasn't making a mistake. He looked a very presentable young man, but one could never be really sure.

Johnny made his way to the top floor where the restaurant was situated. He sat down in the non-smoking area whilst fiddling with the menu, and before he had chance to order anything, he heard, "Johnny, Johnny, I'm so sorry." It was Sue. She hurriedly made her way towards him. She had a slight smile and was dressed in a sloppy yellow jumper and a pair of baggy track-suit bottoms and trainers, but to Johnny she looked even more beautiful than she had done the previous day.

"I'm so sorry about last night," she went on. "You see, when I got home, there was a message left for me, to tell me that my Dad had been rushed into hospital. I went straight to the hospital. I thought of 'phoning the Five Bells but didn't have enough change to find the number from directory enquiries. I was up there for ages," she gabbled on without taking a breath.

"What's the matter with your Dad?" Johnny asked trying to sound sympathetic and also trying to make her slow down a bit.

"Oh, he's all right now, he had a bad attack of Asthma. He's home now but we didn't get out of there until well past midnight."

"Basildon Hospital?" Johnny enquired.

"Yes."

"You mean to tell me, you were only a few hundred yards away from the Five Bells and I was sitting there all by myself, getting drunk and feeling miserable? If I had known, I could have brought you a drink up and we could have got drunk together," said Johnny, trying to make light of the situation.

The two laughed together and Johnny felt enormously relieved. He realised that he hadn't been stood up intentionally. This made him feel much better. They made arrangements to meet when Sue finished work that afternoon. He couldn't take his eyes off her.

Having got over the initial misunderstanding, the two were a big hit with one another, they spent a lot of time together and the rest of Johnny's holiday in each other's company.

Although he loved his job, whilst he was away he could not stop thinking about her and he couldn't wait to get home to be with her again. When he did come home he would play tricks on her like phoning her, making out he was miles away, when all the time he was outside Liberty's. She never knew what to expect. He was very unpredictable. On several occasions he turned up at her house at Vange and surprised her. She was always very pleased to see him. He became almost as well known at Liberty's as Sue, by the other members of the staff, because Sue was always talking about her Johnny. She had fallen for him in a big way. They made a handsome couple.

Chapter 3.

They courted for just over two years. The courtship, although very loving and romantic, was never smooth. Sue didn't like Johnny working away from home, especially overseas and Johnny wasn't too keen on her working in London. They suffered their frustration, they both worked very hard and eventually they had saved enough money to put a deposit down on their own house. Johnny didn't get on with her parents. He never really got to know them and because of his stand-offish attitude, Sue's parents formed an unfavourable opinion of Johnny. They agreed with their daughter, Johnny shouldn't be working overseas. After many arguments, Johnny started to look for work a little nearer home just to keep the peace. He enjoyed his job and was perfectly happy in doing what he was doing, but to keep their romance on an even keel, he took a job at a small engineering company at Wickford, where he was employed as a turner, operating a lathe. He knew it would only be temporary, but it kept Sue happy. He was not travelling all over the world and she was able to see him every evening.

They were married in the registry office at Grays without much fuss. It was Sue's big day and although she would have liked a big posh wedding, she was happy and the money they saved by being sensible would go towards their new home. The wedding breakfast was held at the Commodore Public house, quite near to where Sue's parents lived. The couple, intent on making their marriage work and determined to start life together the way they wanted it to carry on, flew off to Fuengirola, on the south coast of Spain, for their honeymoon. Their time in Spain was probably the happiest time that they had spent together. They were on their own and they only had one another to worry about. Johnny made a lot of fuss of her and she, in turn, would mollycoddle her new husband. They were extremely happy together and made the most of the first few days. They knew that when they got home their lives would become more difficult, money was going to be tight, the mortgage would have to be paid and their new home required furnishing.

They had done everything properly, they had their honeymoon and the time had come to move into their new home. The house they were lucky enough to purchase was situated in Chadwell, a small town not far from Vange. Not far enough for Johnny, he still didn't see eye to eye with Sue's parents. 'Still,' he thought to himself, 'I haven't married the parents;' and was very happy with his young, beautiful bride. The house was in Orchard Road, a nice, quiet area with nice, quality houses. Sue's parents couldn't understand how a young couple like them could afford such a nice house, after all they had been married for years and were still living in a council house. That was part of the problem. It was their attitude that Johnny didn't like, they were small-minded and had no real ambition. Her Dad was a bus driver and was quite content with his life, until he saw someone doing well, and then he couldn't understand why he hadn't been able to get so much out of life. He was very outspoken in his rather small-minded way.

The house was detached and the one next door was exactly the same, but the opposite way round. It had a garage and plenty of room to park extra cars in the driveway. The two houses, though detached, stood side by side, separated only by a privet hedge that had grown to a great height between the two gardens, but had been regularly cut at the front of the houses. The pair of houses were the only two like it in the street and had, at one time, been decorated identically, but now the newly acquired house of Sue and Johnny's needed a coat of paint, whilst the one next door was immaculate. They both had one bay window and a half-tiled, facing wall that made both houses look much older than they really were. The garden was a good size, a bit too big for Johnny, he had no interest in gardening, but because the house was new to them, was prepared to have a go. As long as the garden looked tidy and the grass was kept short, it would keep Sue happy. Flowers and the like could come later.

They moved in with very little furniture and were going to have to furnish their new home gradually. They received a considerable amount of help from their new neighbours, who had lived in the identical house next door for many years. Their names were Ron and Brenda. Brenda was a full time housewife and Ron was a salesman who worked in a departmental store selling electrical appliances. They had two teenage boys, and were a good few years older than Sue and Johnny. Ron's garden was immaculate, he was obviously a bit of an expert gardener.

Sue and Brenda became great mates. Johnny and Ron didn't get quite so close but they often passed the time of day together. Old Ron was very good to the young couple, he helped Johnny with the gardening and the odd bit of decorating. He liked Sue very much but Johnny he could take or leave, there always seemed to be an air of the show-off about Johnny and he always tried to act with an air of superiority.

Johnny would run Sue to the station every morning, in the car, to catch the early train. She had to be at work at nine o'clock, which meant that she had to catch the eight o'clock train every morning to enable her to get to Regent Street on time. Johnny would then drive on to his job at Wickford. Sue would make her own way home from the station in the evenings as quite often Johnny would get involved in working overtime and wasn't always able to meet her at the station. Brenda would often pop next door to see Sue before Johnny got home. They became firm friends and Brenda would very often prepare something for their tea to save Sue the trouble of cooking when she got home from working all day in London.

Johnny wasn't very happy with his job or the money it paid. He started to become discontented and he took to fetching home small amounts of brass scrap and off cuts which he saved in his garage until there was enough to take to the scrap man to sell to supplement his income. Sue wasn't keen on Johnny stealing from his employer, although it was only scrap, and they had many heated discussions over it, Johnny always saying that it was part of the job and that he was entitled to the scrap. Sue knew different.

Whilst reading the local newspaper during one of Johnny's weekend breaks, he noticed an advertisement in the Situations Vacant column. It was advertising for a salesman to promote laser profile cutting. He excitedly showed Sue, who agreed that it was more his cup of tea than operating a lathe. He applied for the job and, much to his surprise, was successful in his application. The position was working for a company that had just started up in the laser profile cutting industry. It was a bit more hi-tech than anything he had done before, but he was very keen and pretty versatile. The company was Precision Laser Ltd and its premises were at Purfleet, which was the industrial area of the market town of Grays.

The company was fairly newly established and everyone who was employed there was extremely full of enthusiasm and determined to make the firm a success, which in turn gave the whole place a nice atmosphere. Johnny was issued with a company car, his salary was greatly increased, but in turn he had to work much harder and put a lot more hours in. He really got involved with the job, he loved his work and he found out that the chap who had done the job before him had been sacked for dishonesty and not producing results. He had spent more time looking after his several rented accommodations than actually going out and looking for new business. Johnny took no notice of what had happened before he joined the company. He had now got himself a good job, with company car and a certain amount of status, and nothing was going to stop him rubbing Sue's father's face in it.

Sue wasn't keen on Johnny being away at nights which he often had to do. She would often invite Brenda over from next door for the evening to keep her company, especially if Ron was out at his snooker club. They would chat about a variety of things. Sue would sometimes open up her heart to Brenda, about her fears that Johnny wasn't the man that she thought she had married and she feared that he was having an affair, no proof, just woman's intuition. Brenda tried to comfort her and give her the necessary support to allay her fears. Sue appreciated Brenda's company but inwardly she was becoming more and more unhappy. Her marriage wasn't working out quite like she thought it would.

When Johnny was at home he had taken to going out most evenings to the local public houses and often came home late and sometimes very drunk. Sue started to go out with him, thinking to herself that if you can't beat them, then you must join them, but she didn't like the company he kept, or the places he went and gave up keeping him company at his unsavoury haunts. This suited Johnny as he felt that Sue cramped his style. One evening he was out and Sue was doing the washing. She discovered lipstick on the sleeve of one of his shirts. She showed it to Brenda and Brenda had to agree that it most certainly was lipstick. Sue waited until Johnny was sober and was sure that he understood what he was being accused of.

It did no good, all she got for an answer was "don't be so bloody daft, woman." The fact that she was questioning him made him mad and aggressive. He hated feeling as though he was being checked up on and went into one of his moods. Johnny wasn't putting the effort into his marriage that he had done when they were first married and spent more and more time out of the house at the local pubs.

Sue gradually became more and more suspicious and resorted to regularly going through his pockets. It soon became very apparent that he was, indeed, seeing someone else. She found a packet of condoms in his pocket one evening, in his suit that he had taken off just prior to going to get bathed before he went out. Sue was gutted. In their marriage they didn't use such things. She was very upset at having found the proof that she hoped she never would and certainly wasn't going to stand for such goings on. She sat and waited for him to come home. When he eventually arrived home in a semi-drunken state, she tackled him about what she had found in his pockets. He became extremely abusive and lost his temper and the outcome was a terrible fight, Sue coming off much the worse. Sue ended up in hospital, pretty badly beaten up. She never forgave him and no matter what he said or did, she would not return home. She had lost faith in him and because she could no longer trust him, decided to separate, if only to see whether Johnny could pull himself together, inwardly feeling that the marriage was over.

She moved back to her parents' home, much to Johnny's disgust. No way were they going to have the last laugh. He did as he liked and brought many different women home with him now that he had the house to himself. This was frowned upon by Brenda, who would relate to Ron every time she saw someone different arriving or leaving.

Having ruined his marriage, he put a big effort into his job and became very successful. Really, he could do anything if he put his mind to it. Before long his hard work paid off. He became an integral part of the team at Precision Laser Ltd and was greatly appreciated by the management. He tried on more than one occasion to contact Sue and maybe patch things up. He realised what a fool he had been but Sue, taking advice from her family, wouldn't have anything to do with him.

Several months passed. Sue was still living at home with her parents. Johnny received a letter from a firm of solicitors, T.C. Jorden and Partners. The letter was informing him that divorce proceedings were being prepared against him. He knew that her parents were most likely behind it. The letter went on to say that Mrs Susan

Gibbs was demanding her share of the property at Orchard Road and half the contents of the marital home, plus a share of the savings, and maintenance money as well. Johnny read the letter with a lump in his throat. He never really expected it to come to that. After studying the letter for some time, he screwed it up and threw it away. No way was that bitch or her family going to get their hands on his house.

As a result of Johnny's complete lack of co-operation, and his failing to answer any correspondence, the divorce hearing went ahead in his absence. T.C. Jorden's company of solicitors did their job well and were awarded by the court everything that they had claimed on their client's behalf. Johnny was given time to sell the house and time to make good the other claims.

The house was put on the market. Johnny would not permit any For Sale boards to be erected outside the house and the price he arranged with the estate agents was of such a nature that the sale would have been very difficult to complete. He did let Sue help herself to any of the contents of the home that she felt she needed. Brenda helped her with the furniture while Johnny was at work. During her two or three visits to collect various items, Brenda was pleased to learn that Sue had been promoted in her job and that she had found herself a flat in North London and was making a new start for herself.

Johnny eventually found out where she lived and, as she was out of reach of the rest of her family, often called to see her, either while going to or returning from calls he was making on behalf of the company. At first she wasn't too disappointed to see him, but then it became more regular and sometimes he would turn up at the flat drunk and argumentative and she had to put a stop to it.

She eventually had to get a Court Order to keep him away, but Johnny always thought he was above the law and took little notice. That is, until the police were called one evening, when he was making a particular nuisance of himself and he was arrested. When he appeared in Court before the magistrate he was given one final warning and it was made quite clear to him that he must keep away from his ex-wife or suffer the consequences.

Johnny knuckled down and obeyed the instructions from the Court, at first. The house remained on the market and Johnny kept up the repayments on the mortgage. Although a few people came to view the premises, he had no intentions of selling it. Then, unfortunately, the housing market slumped and for a couple years the prices of property fell. The chance of selling the house became very remote. He didn't keep the place well maintained and eventually it had to be re-valued. After much thought and deliberation he made Sue an offer through her solicitors, which she accepted, although he hadn't got anywhere near the amount of money that he offered. A deal was worked out and he started sending her small amounts of money on a very irregular basis. When he did have a reasonable amount to send her, he broke the court order and took it to her personally. She didn't make a fuss about it. All the time he behaved himself she didn't mind.

Whilst trying to make a new life for herself, Sue had met a man of her own age and in similar circumstances. He happened to be at Sue's flat one evening when Johnny called to make a payment to her. Johnny was furious. He was either bloody-minded or extremely jealous. He made the poor bloke's life hell. Sue had to ask Johnny to leave. He did, knowing that he could not afford to have the police involved but promised that if the chap was ever there again, he would stop all payments for the house. He didn't go to see Sue again for a very long time.

After a few months, he started to make a lot of money. He sent Sue payments on a regular basis by post and even she was surprised by the regularity of the payments and even more surprised at the amounts that arrived each time. She surmised that he must be doing very well at his job.

Johnny realised that he had made a terrible mistake with Sue. He was still very fond of her and couldn't stop thinking about her. The thought of her with someone else played on his mind. If only he could turn the clock back, things could have been so different. He tried desperately to forget her by putting all his energy into his work, which he succeeded in doing for some time.

He made several friends and acquaintances whilst working for Precision Laser Ltd. One chap in particular was the son of the owner of a small steel stockists. His name was Bart Tornton. He made friends with Johnny and took him under his wing, took him out on the town, introduced him to a variety of beautiful women and even helped him get membership at the very prestigious Tennis Club at Romford. They remained good pals but Johnny had trouble keeping up with Bart who always seemed to have an endless supply of money, so unfortunately Johnny had to cool the friendship slightly. The two men stayed in touch with one another. Bart helped Johnny to forget what had happened between him and Sue and, as they got to know each other a little better, showed him an easy way to make some extra money, although not exactly legally.

Chapter 4.

Several years later. It was the first of August, a typical hot English summer's day, not a breath of air and not a cloud in the sky. Only the twin tracer trail of an airliner, off to some distant, exotic resort, was visible in the otherwise clear, blue sky. The heat had built up so that every movement became a chore and increased the amount of sweat that would run down Ron's face. Ron had been up early to water his flowers and tend his small vegetable patch and do his general pottering about before the heat of the day could affect him. He was on his way home from doing his daily trudge to the local newsagent with his old faithful dog, Ben. Ben was a mongrel, but he showed more Labrador in his make up than any other breed. He had been jet black but now grey tinges were showing his years. The heat hit Ben more than it did Ron. The dog dawdled by his side, making his own pace and panting and slobbering with his dribbling tongue hanging at the side of his mouth, as if every step was too much trouble.

"Soon be home, boy," Ron said as he walked in time with the dog knowing that as soon as they were home, the poor old boy would collapse in the shade of one of the tall conifers in the rear garden at the back of their home in Orchard Road and probably sleep for the rest of the afternoon.

Ron was a man in his early fifties, slightly overweight, especially in the stomach area as a result of the regular two or three pints of best bitter consumed on a regular basis. He was slightly balding and although he would have liked to have kept his hair, he didn't really care. He tried to keep himself fit, but was the first to admit that exercise was not high on the list of his priorities. In fact, the most exercise he had was walking round the snooker table at his social club where most of his mates seemed to be the same shape. Ron had a great passion for snooker and, for the amount of practice he had, he would be the first to admit that he wasn't particularly good at it.

Brenda was Ron's wife of some twenty six years. Ron was her hero, she pampered him at every opportunity, indeed she was one of the main reasons why he had trouble controlling his weight. Brenda was about a year younger than Ron. She felt it was her duty to feed him and make sure a meal was available at meal times whether Ron was hungry or not. She carried her age very well, her figure was slim, she had lovely hazel eyes, which were clear and bright, her hair was natural blonde but not as bright as it used to be, and she, by anybody's standards, was a very attractive woman. Ron knew this and was very proud of his wife and, indeed, deemed himself a very lucky man.

On reaching home it was Ron's usual routine to sit and take coffee with Brenda and let Ben recuperate in the garden, although it was only when the temperature was high that Ben needed a rest. Ron would sit in the cool of the house and while his time away doing the cross-word, checking the answers from the previous day's puzzle. Whilst reading his paper, his attention was drawn to the fact that it was the first of August, the first of August was the day of the year when the new registration for motor vehicles was introduced, changing the prefix letter on the number plates. He could do with a new car but the one he had was going to have to do for the time being. His car had seen better days and to be fair it had never let him down and the big bonus was that it was paid for. With all the time he had on his hands of late, he had used some of it to make his old car look immaculate and now it was all polished up, he

23

didn't use it unless it was essential. His purse strings were tight, which meant he really couldn't afford the cost of the fuel to make the thing go.

"Shut up, Ben, you silly old fool! You're always the same as soon as the postman comes up the path. Lay down!" said Ron, to his faithful, old, black mutt, who had been his mate for many a long year. Ben had been the dog his two sons had reared in their teens, but as they got older and left home, they had left the dog with their parents to look after. He was pretty old in doggy terms, but in fact he was thirteen years old, and a regular old gentleman, and now neither Brenda nor Ron would ever think of losing him.

Brenda retrieved the letter from the mat, knowing exactly what it contained, and passing it to Ron said, "It's arrived, so later, when it cools a bit, you can take Ben and go and get some bits from the Mini Mart." Ron didn't open the letter, he also knew what it was. He knew that as long as he signed on, every other Thursday, as regular as clockwork, he would receive his ninety-six pounds and forty-eight pence from the establishment, as a reward for the twenty-odd years he had worked before he had been made redundant. He looked on it as some sort of reward for the service he had put in. He had always been conscientious and was dumbfounded when the crunch came, making Brenda's and his lives a bit of a struggle. It wasn't their only income, Ron had elected to draw the small pension he was entitled to from the company he had worked for, which wasn't enough to live on, but enabled him to have his first ever break from work in his life. Their life wasn't that bad really. Their car, though old, was paid for, they had no mortgage to speak of and the lump sum redundancy payment was tucked away safely in a short term investment, waiting for Ron to get another job. He had made many applications for jobs and wasn't having much luck. He hadn't pushed too hard and was content to let the summer go by before really getting down to work searching. The only problem for the both of them was trying to keep up appearances at the social club, where he played snooker. What they hadn't realised was that, when there isn't a regular wage coming in at the end of each month, you can't carry on being Mr Big and buying everyone drinks. Indeed, the people you had been particularly generous to over the years, seemed to have disappeared now that money was becoming a little tight.

They lived in a quiet road, quite a nice property. Although considered a country area, it was, over the last few years, becoming very rural. It was south Essex and a small town called Chadwell, about twenty five miles from London. The nearest real town was Basildon, although Lakeside was up and coming. Not much real industry, but work was there, if you looked for it.

Being on the north of the River Thames, most of Ron's acquaintances and friends were employed either by the big Ford Motor Company, at Dagenham, or Basildon, where Ford produced tractors, or in the docks at Tilbury. Ron had been in retail, but he was hoping for a change.

"Come on Boy" said Ron, as he got the dog's lead from the drawer in the kitchen. Ben recognised the signal and started yapping, squeaking and wagging his tail and making all sorts of fuss. "Let's go and cash this Giro," as if the dog could understand. Ben started pulling and getting excited as usual until about a hundred yards down the road, when his years caught up and he settled down and behaved like the perfect old gentleman that he was. The ritual of getting excited, every time the lead was shown to him, stemmed from the time when Ben was a pup. When the two sons of Ron and Brenda, would take him out on the rare occasions when they weren't off courting or playing football, when they would tease him and ask him to go and find the lead.

It wasn't far to the General Post Office and it gave Ron a chance to view the other properties in the road as they walked. Ron, having had plenty of time on his hands of late, was completely up to date with all his chores, and would compare the paint-work and the gardens of the other properties. A warm glow would come over him, knowing that in his own mind his garden was one of the best in the road.

Having cashed the Giro, he was under orders to visit the local Mini Mart to do Brenda's bit of shopping and, leaving Ben tied to the doggy rail, he went inside and collected the few items she wanted that were itemised on a small list. He packed them into a plastic carrier bag and made ready to return home. Walking around the small shopping centre, with old Ben in tow, gave Ron the chance to meet some of his acquaintances from his club, and some of his old customers from his retail days. He could spend quite a time on a sunny afternoon just chatting, about nothing in particular, to friends with old Ben at his side, indeed Ben was usually the topic of conversation. As soon as Ron stopped to chat, Ben would lay down on the ground and patiently wait until his master had stopped chatting, before he would stand and, with his master's permission, head for home.

Chapter 5

Returning home by way of the common, he let Ben off the lead, but the old dog didn't leave Ron's side. He was still getting over the walk he had earlier in the day, and as it was still very warm he was content just to dawdle at Ron's side. Leaving the common, as they approached their house, Ron's attention was drawn to the brand spanking-new, gleaming-red, open-top sports car standing in the drive of the house next door, and there was Johnny standing and admiring his new acquisition, duster in hand, wiping off the very smallest pieces of dust.

"Hi, Ron," he shouted, inviting a comment from Ron about the car. They weren't exactly friends, but had passed the time of day together on the odd occasion, especially when Brenda was friendly with Susan his ex-wife.

"What have you got there? Blimey, have you won the pools?" said Ron as he walked towards Johnny's drive, not taking his eyes off the car.

"That's nice," Ron said, as Ben sniffed one of the tyres and lifted his head and exhaled powerfully through his nostrils, as though he had smelt something distasteful.

"Sit boy!" said Ron, as he patted Ben's head. "That is nice Johnny, that'll be a head turner, I bet that cost you a pretty penny."

"Yes! I've always wanted one and, as things are improving at work, I thought what the hell, why not? You only live once." Johnny carried on in a world of his own, explaining all the ins and outs of his new gleaming machine. Ron wasn't really listening, but inside he did admire the new sparkling motor standing in front of him, and with a touch of envy. He tried not to show too much enthusiasm.

"What's happening at work then mate, you say things are picking up?"

"Yes," replied Johnny. "We've been busy for the last few months, we're doing a lot of work for the Ministry of Defence, and we're expanding, we've taken on new premises at Lower Street, you know the old Motor Factor Distribution Plant, we move in there next month. The inside is a bit of a mess and requires a lot of work, but they have put a team in there to clean and paint it and they are making a pretty good job of it. I was down there yesterday and I reckon it's over double the size we've got now."

"Really?" Ron grunted, his ears pricking up, thinking to himself that there might be a chance of a job. He listened patiently to every word that Johnny uttered.

Johnny continued, "I won't be going there yet, but I believe it's on the cards that everything will be moved there eventually."

Ron hadn't taken his eyes off the new motor and, still looking down at the immaculate piece of machinery in front of him, said, "I don't suppose they are going to need any more staff, are they? I'm getting a bit browned off being at home."

Johnny stood and pondered Ron's question, then answered, "Yes they are. I know for a fact that they are taking on at least four more operators. I don't think that that would suit you, but I know they are going to need someone in the production office. If you like, I'll make some enquiries and let you know, or," he stood and thought for a moment, "I'll tell you what, phone Mr Bill Ross, at Purfleet. He's the boss, ask for an application form and in the meantime, I'll see him and tell him that I know you, I'll put a word in for you. I'm sure the job in the production office will be right up your street, it's mainly paperwork but I know you will be able to handle it, you've already done a bit of pen pushing."

"That would be smashing, Johnny. I'll do that and I'll let you know how I get on." Ron turned to walk away, giving Ben a gentle tug, clutching his plastic bag of shopping, turned his head over his shoulder, and said, "Great! Thanks Johnny, I'll give him a ring." As he moved away he called back, "I like your car." Ron hurriedly opened the front door, slipped the lead off Ben's head and put the shopping in the kitchen. He called out of the back door.

"Bren, Bren, here, I've something to tell you."

She came in from the garden, smiling. "Yes, yes, I know, I've seen you out there with him. It's a bit on the flash side for him isn't it,"

"No, not that, old Johnny-boy reckons there is a job going at his firm, at Lower Street. Wouldn't that be great? Lower Street is easily within walking distance," Ron said excitedly.

"Yes, but what sort of job is it?"

"Pen pushing, as far as I can make out. He works for Precision Laser, he's going to have a word with his boss and I'm going to phone for an application form."

"Go on then," Brenda replied. "It can't do any harm, but do you know anything about that sort of trade?"

"I'm not stupid, I can soon pick things up, besides there's bound to be some sort of training," Ron blurted out, trying to give Brenda some reassurance, knowing inwardly that he wasn't as confident as he would have Brenda believe. Ron had for the best part of his life been in the retail trade, although in his younger days he had worked in engineering for an agricultural machinery manufacturers. Retail had been his life for the last twenty-odd years, he had specialised in electrical but the company he had worked for was part of a major industrial company. They, after many years, had decide to pull out of retail, thus making Ron and many others redundant.

Ron had enjoyed the last few months at home, but knowing that the summer would soon be over, and that the list of his promised chores was nearing the end, the thought of autumn and winter ahead didn't fill him with excitement. The thought of a job locally and within walking distance, did appeal to him. He scoured the local paper as usual and found in the situations vacant column the advert referring to the vacancies that John had spoke about. He phoned for an application form and was eagerly awaiting for the document to arrive.

Chapter 6

Ron had not been able to speak to Mr Ross, at the Purfleet Depot, but as promised by his secretary, the application form had arrived, and duly completed, been returned. The morning of the interview had arrived, his interview was at eleven-thirty. Ron, all smartly dressed in his best suit, crisp white shirt, tie and shiny shoes, and inspected by Brenda before leaving home, was sitting in the office waiting for Mr Ross to arrive. He was on his way from Lower Street, he had been told, and would not be very long. Ron's eyes gazed around the office in which he sat, not very tidy he thought to himself, the desk was tidy but it was obvious that the desk top had been cleared for the purpose of the interview. The desk-top deluge was deposited in various sites around the office. There were two computers in the office, one was turned on and on the screen was a series of triangular patterns being displayed as a screen saver. On the wall, in what looked like brass, was a large symbol showing that Precision Laser Ltd was, in fact, attributed with the British Standards Certificate. Ron was just wondering to himself what that really meant, when the door was pushed open and in walked a young man in his early thirties. His face was covered in grease smudges and he was dressed in a pair of dark green overalls which were pretty dirty.

A hand was thrust towards Ron and with a big smile, Mr Bill Ross said "I'm sorry to keep you waiting. I expect Johnny Gibbs has told you we are trying to get Lower Street up and running."

Ron shook his hand and answered nervously. "Yes, Johnny did mention it," and thought to himself 'this chap's a bit young, I expect he's some sort of whiz kid, or something of that nature.'

Bill Ross was, in fact, only thirty-three. He had, in his early life, gone to college to study engineering. He had worked in many countries as a service engineer, for a company that sold and installed laser-cutting machines. Seeing the potential for making money he had mortgaged himself up to the hilt to buy one of these complicated machines to start his own company. After a lot of initial success, the company was expanding quite rapidly and he had gone into other types of sub contract work, like sheet metal work, turning and welding. His latest venture, Lower Street, was, in fact, a move to accommodate everything under one roof and he had purchased the premises on mortgage, and it was going to be quite a gamble to make it pay but he knew that one day if, God willing, everything went according to plan and the venture was a success, he would be very wealthy. He had got a good team around him and he was paying top dollar for the right people. Most of the staff that helped him start the company were still employed there. He had earned their respect and he was a good boss. He was very articulate in his manner. Although he was in overalls, they fitted him perfectly, and Ron thought to himself this young man would look good in whatever he wore.

After chatting for a few minutes, it was quite obvious that Bill Ross did, indeed, know what he was talking about, and Ron could see that the man had an air of authority about him, and the fact that both men spoke the same language helped the interview along at an interesting level of conversation. Ron soon realised that the job in question was going to be offered to him, and any apprehension he had was quickly being lost. Bill Ross hardly mentioned Johnny Gibbs, only in passing, and Ron soon realised that the pen-pushing job was going to be a real hands-on position and going to need a lot of hard work. He was beginning to feel some excitement about the prospect of starting his new job and getting back into a regular daily routine. The salary, to Ron, was of little importance, it was the chance to start a new job that he needed. He was happy with the opportunity to be working, especially locally, and especially as it would be within walking distance from home. He was very pleasantly surprised to find that, in fact, he would be receiving about fifteen thousand pounds a year in wages, something along the lines he had been used to at his previous job. With his redundancy money safely invested and now a regular wage about to come in again, his and Brenda's financial status was beginning to look up.

"Mr Ross," as Ron called the young executive, "Thank you very much for your time, I'm happy to start next month, and let's hope our acquaintance will be profitable to us both."

"I'm sure it will be," came the smiling reply back. He said "Look forward to seeing you on Monday, the first of next month. You will report to Mr Sharp, Mr Brian Sharp, he is the production manager and he will set you to work. It will be part of your duties to give him every bit of assistance you can and try and take some of the weight off his shoulders. With the bigger plant and the extra machines, I'm sure he is going to have his work cut out, coping with the extra work load."

"Fine, well, thanks once again," Ron said as he got up, feeling, without anybody saying anything, that the meeting was over.

They once more shook hands and bid each other the time of day. Ron set off back to his car feeling absolutely exhilarated and a bit apprehensive, not really knowing what the job entailed and if he was going to be suitable or not. He certainly had got something to tell Brenda. It looked as though things for the two of them were on the up and up.

Chapter 7

Three months had passed since Ron had started at Lower Street, the time had flown by and Ron had got into a sort of routine every day. He would walk to work nearly every day, unless it was raining, carrying his sandwiches that had been lovingly made by Brenda. He took sandwiches because lunch breaks were limited to half an hour which didn't really give him time to get home and back for the midday break and Brenda would make sure that he had a proper meal when he got home in the evening.

He was feeling quite content inside. He felt that he had made quite a lot of progress in the short time he had been at Precision Laser Ltd. Not having much experience in the engineering trade of late, he found the trade jargon a little slow to understand and the reading of drawings extremely difficult but, having explained to the others in the office his problem, they had helped him and he, being very quick to learn, seemed to fit in pretty well.

The factory at Lower Street was an old building. It had been completely modernised by gutting the place and rebuilding the inside to accommodate the large laser cutting machines. There were two groups of offices, one was the production office block, which was adjacent to the shop floor, whilst the other block, which had its own car park and housed all the administration departments was at the front of the building and completely separate from the main factory block.

There were three others working in the same office as Ron, Brian Sharp, the floor manager, or to give him his proper title, Production Manager, Franco and Robby. Their desks were placed in two batches of two, Ron and Brian Sharp sat opposite one another, and at the other end of the office sat Robby and Franco facing each other. The office was quite large with windows running the whole length of one side. There was a small room off the office which was used to house the Photostat machine, and the out-going fax machine. There were three doors that opened into the office. One leading to the dispatch area, one leading to the executive office block and the third led to the workshop floor

Franco and Robby's jobs were to quote from drawings for prices, to produce all sorts of profile cutting, welding, turning, and bending in the manufacture of components for all sorts of trades. It sounds very complicated but in fact every thing was worked out with the aid of computers, of which were four in the office, one each. Robby's and Franco's were used exclusively for quoting, Brian's and Ron's although they could be used for quoting, were mainly used for producing the job cards for the machine operators to work from.

Robby was the clever one. He had done an apprenticeship as a draughtsman and was teaching Franco as much as he could. He was very abrupt in his manner and didn't suffer fools gladly. He was tall, very lean, always hungry and very full of himself. He was one of the most sarcastic people Ron had ever come across for a man of thirty-five or thereabouts. He was very moody and when he was depressed, no-one could ask him a question without taking a fair amount of verbal abuse. He was married with three children, aged from eleven to fifteen and, from the sound of it, they were quite a handful. One thing that Robby was good at was to keep a record of the number of days he had been off work sick. He had many days off, but not too many that he could be put on the carpet. His complexion was very sallow and when he wanted anyone to feel sorry for him he could act better than any professional actor.

Franco, on the other hand, was quite short, stocky, not much hair, and about the same age as Robby and, as Ron had discovered, a bit on the lazy side. He would put more effort into trying to get out of doing a job than actually getting down and doing it, but to be fair, he had been an enormous help to Ron during those first few weeks. He was a moaning little chap. If Robby was to have a new pen or scrap pad, Franco had to have one as well and he could sit for hours tapping his computer keys, making out he was working, for the benefit of Brian (Porkie). Franco was also married but had no children. He could make Robby upset at the drop of a hat by asking questions that had an obvious answer, but they seemed to get on well with one another, nevertheless.

Brian Sharp sat opposite Ron, a man probably a little older than Ron, about his early to middle fifties, big, slightly overweight and, as Ron thought, a bit on the crude side. He hadn't got a good command of the Queen's English. He was an ex-Staff Sergeant in the Royal Electrical and Mechanical Engineers and never let anybody forget it. He would bring the army into every conversation whenever he could. What he couldn't see was the heads being tossed in the air behind his back, whenever he started one of his army stories, but must have noticed how quickly the room would empty once he had started. His personal habits left a lot to be desired, he could belch, fart, pick his nose, shout and swear, without the slightest consideration for those who worked with and around him. He was also a bit of a bully to two or three of the lads on the shop floor who hadn't got the guts to stand up to him. One lad in particular, who had a slight stutter, would take most of the foul language and shouting, but always managed to keep a wry smile on his face, as if to say, I know I can wind you up mate but you'll never get the better of me. Ron admired that little bit of devilment in the lad. On Brian's desk, in a place of honour, was a photograph of himself in full dress uniform, taken in the days when his body was correctly proportioned and, to be fair, he had been a good-looking young man. He had got a pension from the army and he had met his wife whilst serving overseas in Singapore. She was of Oriental descent and they had between them two girls, who were in their early twenties.

There were about forty people altogether, including the night shift, working at Lower Street, and it particularly struck Ron's attention how enthusiastic everyone was. Not many firms with that amount of staff would run so smoothly, with so little supervision. Nearly everyone referred to Brian as Porkie, probably because of his size and his manner, but nobody called him that to his face.

For the most part Ron got on very well with Brian, (Porkie), both men being of nearly the same age. They seemed to have more in common with each other than with the other two in the office, although Brian's, (Porkie's), training of Ron left a lot to be desired. Ron was taught far more by the other two lads in the office. The office floor was carpeted, but the entrance to the shop floor door area was filthy and discoloured. Every time someone came to the office from the shop floor they would trudge black oil, off the metal and filings, into the otherwise clean area, causing Porkie to exercise his lungs and foul language power.

Ron's duties were to collate the drawings with the specific jobs, make sure that the raw materials were ordered and in stock and to meet the delivery dates requested on the purchase orders. Ron really took his job seriously and, to be truthful, did mentally take his job home with him, but as he got more used to it, things did seem to become easier. He made several friends on the telephone during his daily routine of phoning round to get prices and delivery dates and, indeed, most of the suppliers preferred to talk to Ron rather that Porkie. They knew they got the truth from Ron, as Ron's enquiries were always genuine with no exaggeration in quantities to get the price down.

Chapter 8

Ron walked the ten minutes to work at eight-fifteen. 'Tuesday morning,' he thought to himself. 'It won't be long before it's dark at this time in the morning' and added to his thought, 'I'll fetch the car if this chill keeps up.' Nearly dropping Brenda's precious sandwiches he turned his coat collar up to keep out the wind. Due to the drop in temperature he was getting to work in quicker time as he stepped it out to ward off the little nip in the air. As he turned the corner into the plant yard, he noticed the face of Steve, the night supervisor looking out of the production office window. As he drew nearer he could see that the look on Steve's face was a little strained. On entering the office block Ron was thankful that the heating was on. Removing his coat or, better description, anorak, he hung it up on the clothes pegs provided at the far end of the office.

"Ron," said Steve. "The material for the Watkin's job, you know the oversize sheets? We did have it in, I know, because I've found the steel stockist's packing note stating thirty-four, sheets of six mil. but I've got nowhere near enough to finish the job. I'm about ten sheets short. Have you given permission for it to be used on another job?"

Ron thought for a moment, trying to get his brain in gear.

"No, there should be plenty, we've not had any six mil. jobs since the middle of last week, and I know that material for Watkin's only came in on Friday."

"Well, I'm telling you, there ain't enough," Steve replied. "It can't just disappear. According to the packing note, thirty-four sheets were delivered and signed for by the fork-lift driver, and it bloody well ain't here now. It's supposed to be cut and delivered by this afternoon and unless you can get some more material here this morning I'm going to have to break the machine down and finish it later in the week." He continued, cursing and spitting nails. "It's the second time this week that we have been short of material. Something is going drastically wrong with the ordering of material and you've got to get to the bottom of it or I'm going to see the boss."

"OK, mate, give me a couple of minutes, I'll just hang on for Porkie to see if he can throw some light on it."

Ron carried on racking his brains, but couldn't throw any light on it. He couldn't come up with any logical explanation.

By this time, the two lads had arrived. Knowing something was wrong they went onto the shop floor and proceeded to search for the missing material, to no avail.

All of a sudden, "What the bloody hell is going on?" A voice boomed out. Porkie had arrived and, realising that something was wrong and feeling left in the dark, started to go through his normal tantrum, shouting and swearing.

Ron proceeded to explain the problem, to try and calm him down.

"Right," said Porkie to Ron in his usual piggish way. "Drop what you are doing, get on to South Essex Steel. They are coming here this morning, ask them, no bloody well, tell them, to put another ten sheets of six mil. on, and add it to our outstanding order. Then fax over another purchase order to cover it."

"OK., I'll do it straight away," replied Ron, thinking to himself, 'why does he get so damned excited, he could get twice as much done if he was to keep calm.'

Still feeling a bit bemused, Ron got on with the morning's work, trying not to let the morning's events worry him. Ten sheets of six mil. at about a hundred pounds a sheet, wasn't to be overlooked too lightly but, knowing that Porkie would get to the bottom of the mystery, he carried on with his work, knowing that, for the moment at least, the panic was over.

Lunch-time had arrived and so had the ten extra sheets of six mil., to complete the Watkin's job. Robby and Franco went out for lunch. Ron had eaten his sandwiches during the morning lunch break and sat at his desk watching Porkie feed his face with a large salad roll. With a mouth full of half chewed food Porkie looked at Ron and said.

"Ron! You know what happened this morning?"

"Yes."

"Well, that's not the first time that that sort of thing has happened since we've been here. I'm sure that the bastards have cocked the job up and got rid of the scrap by dumping it at the bottom of the skip."

"No! What, ten sheets? You would see the mucked up parts in the skips!"

"Yes, I know, but there has got to be an explanation. We can't keep losing steel like this, apart from being damned expensive it makes us look like prats and it takes an awful lot of explaining to the boss."

They both sat and looked at each other, mulling over what had just been said and trying to think of what had gone wrong.

"Oh, by the way Ron, the boss wants to see you in his office this afternoon, at half-past two."

"What for?" Ron asked alarmed.

"I don't know, I think it's something to do with you being here for thirteen weeks, your trial period is up. Nothing to worry about though, he knows you are doing a pretty good job, I've told him."

"Oh, OK., thanks."

The two lads returned from lunch and Ron got his head down and started the afternoon's chores, feeling a little apprehensive about being summoned to the boss's office in view of the morning's events. Ron thought he had better try and think of something to say about the situation before he saw Mr Ross.

Two-thirty came, and Jill, Mr Ross's secretary, phoned

down to say that Mr Ross was ready to see him. Ron rose to go upstairs. He wasn't looking forward to the interview one little bit.

The two lads, not knowing about the meeting, began to take the mickey out of Ron. "Go on, go and get your cards," they jibed. Grinning like a couple of Cheshire Cats as Ron left the office.

Ron just smiled and made his way up to the first floor. He hadn't been up there before and mentally recalled that these offices were much smarter than the ones where he had been interviewed for the job in the first place. 'Much better,' he thought to himself.

As he approached Jill's desk, she said "go in. He is waiting for you, would you like tea or coffee?"

"Tea, please, thank you," Ron replied as he tapped on the door of the office, noticing that every thing was freshly painted and that the office furniture was all brand new. "And no sugar, thanks," he added as he waited for a reply from inside the office.

"Come in!" He recognised Bill Ross's voice. He stood just inside the office door waiting for a sign from the boss before he moved.

"Sit down. I won't keep you a minute," Bill Ross said.

Ron sat on the chair opposite the desk. Bill Ross was punching away on one of the computers on his enormous desk. He didn't even lift his head as Ron sat down, but Ron did notice that the boss had a very expensive smart dark suit on, unlike the first time that the two met, when he was clad in overalls. Ron's eyes wandered round the office. Everything was spick and span and new. There was a place for everything and everything was in its place. The carpet on the floor was a deep blue colour, sumptuous and matched the decor. The vertical blinds were closed and they also matched the carpet. In the corner stood a cold water dispenser that was the same colour as the rest of the furnishings. It reminded Ron of one of those American offices that you see in films. Ron was sitting in a very comfortable chrome framed armchair, of which there were another two, by the water-dispensing machine.

It seemed ages as Ron sat there in silence, apart from the few grunts that came from the direction of Bill Ross's computer.

"Ah ha! That's it," said Bill, then sat in silence, as if he was pondering the result of his work on the machine. Ron had no idea what Bill was working on, the screen of the computer, was facing away from him. The boss's eyes glanced in Ron's direction, the eye contact between the two men was enough to let Ron know that he was not forgotten. Just then, a tap on the door and in came Jill, carrying a tray with two cups on it.

"Tea for you, no sugar, is that right, Ron?" she said. "And coffee for the boss." As she put the drinks down she smiled at both men, turned and left the room, leaving behind a rather sweet smelling aroma in the air, which was certainly different from some of the smells that developed in the production office from time to time.

"Bit smarter than Purfleet," Ron said trying to break the ice.

"Ermm." Bill said, not really listening to what Ron was saying.

Another few minutes passed, neither men saying anything, which seemed like an age to Ron. Then Bill, as if he had only just realised that Ron was there, looked at him, sipped the beverage that Jill had supplied, quickly tidied up the area of the desk immediately in front of him, sat bolt upright and, with a big smile, said "Right! Down to business. Sorry to keep you, Ron, but as you know, your trial period is up and I'm glad to tell you that the reports we've had about you are all very promising. So, as from Monday, it is my intention to make you permanent staff, which will enable you to join our sickness scheme and entitle you to participate in our pension plan. I'm pleased for you, keep up the good work. We could do with a few more people like you."

"Thanks, I will," Ron replied, with a big smile on his face.

Then both of them sat in silence looking at each other,

both waiting for the other to make the first statement.

Ron, feeling a little uncomfortable, moved his chair as if to get up and go, when Bill cleared his throat, looked directly at Ron and said "Ron, before you go, I'm not sure how to say this, but have you noticed anything unusual going on in your office?"

"Like what?"

" I don't know, anything, anything at all, anything that does not fit into the daily running of the production schedules?"

"No, I can't say I have, unless you mean what happened this morning about the missing metal."

That was still playing on Ron's mind.

"Yes, I know about that," said Bill, shaking his head. "Look Ron something is wrong down there. The reason I'm talking to you is that it started long before you joined us. I believe it was going on at the other depot, I don't know what is going on, but I've got to get to the bottom of it."

Ron sat and listened as Bill went through a whole episode of shortages, mucked-up deliveries and missing job cards, all of which Ron had no idea was going on.

"Can I ask you to keep your ears and eyes open? I'm not asking you to rat on your work mates, but there has been an awful lot of unexplained shortages and customers let down over the last six months and I need to know what exactly is going on down there?"

"Well of course, if I can help, I'll be only too glad to." Then, thinking for a few seconds, said, " If I do see something suspicious, who do I report it to, Porkie?" Then realising that he had used Porkie's rather cruel nickname, stopped and said, "I mean Brian Sharp."

Bill smiled, he knew about the nickname, he often used it himself.

"No, not for the time being. Report directly to me, don't tell anybody else until I know who is involved, or even if anybody is involved. I find it hard to believe that any of our staff would be foolish enough to be thieving from us."

"OK., but how will I contact you? I rarely see you to talk

43

to."

"I know, look, I don't like doing this, but you can telephone me at home in the evenings and if anything really urgent comes up, this is my mobile number. I don't normally hand that out, so please don't let the others see it." He handed Ron a small piece of paper on which was written, in pencil, the mobile telephone number. Ron read the small piece of paper and carefully folded it and put it safely away in his wallet.

"Having informed you that I know there is something amiss, Ron, I know that you will be discreet. I don't want anybody to know that I am suspicious."

"That's perfectly understood and I won't contact you unless I have something serious to report."

"O.K., thanks, Ron, I appreciate that." Bill went on, "You see, we must keep it quiet until we can be sure what is causing these discrepancies. Such a lot depends on this place being a success. There is a lot of money invested in this company and the future of us all is hanging in the balance."

The two men sat and chatted for a while, Bill doing most of the talking, but it was quite clear that both men had a mutual respect for one another and that, in fact, both of them had the same interest at heart, that of solving the mystery of the missing materials. Ron felt slightly stupid inside. He felt he should have noticed that something was wrong when in fact he hadn't. He made this known to Bill, and to Ron's surprise, Bill informed Ron that he felt just as stupid, but was informed that from now on, things were going to be looked on in a totally different light. Then, Bill, remembering that he had another engagement and that the meeting with Ron had taken much more time than he had intended, informed Ron that the meeting must come to a close because he had arranged to meet Johnny Gibbs at three o'clock. Looking at the clock on the wall behind Ron, he began to sort the paperwork for the next meeting and said, "Good luck! Keep up the good work, I'll speak to you in a few day's time."

Bill stood and shook Ron's hand and, with a little smile and a wink, Ron turned and as he was leaving said, "Thank you, goodbye."

Closing the door behind him he walked straight into the conversation that Jill and Johnny Gibbs were having as John sat on the edge of Jill's desk.

"Hello, Ron!" exclaimed Johnny, "It's the first time I've seen you since you started here. How are you getting on? I keep meaning to pop round and see you, but I never seem to get the time. Blimey, you'd think as neighbours and working for the same company we would see something of one another?"

"Yes," said Ron, "I do see you drive up the road now and then, Yes I'm doing all right, I must be, Mr Ross has just made my job here permanent," he added, smiling.

" Great!" Johnny replied as he walked to the door of Bill Ross's office. "You and Brenda must come round for a drink one evening. I'll give you a knock."

"Thanks, that will be nice. See you," answered Ron. He smiled at Jill and headed towards the stairs.

John Gibbs was on the sales team. His position was to visit prospective customers, sort out any complaints, sell Precision Laser Ltd. and to supervise the Quality Control department. He had lived next door to Ron and Brenda for over seven years. They had been quite friendly to start with but Johnny and his wife, Susan, had split up some time ago. Johnny hadn't remarried, but had a steady stream of girl friends, much to Brenda's annoyance. She used to get on very well with Susan but after she moved away had lost contact. Ron wasn't sure about the invitation. Johnny had always seemed a bit of a big head to Ron. He dismissed the thought as he smiled at Jill, and made his way back to the stairs that took him to the ground floor. His mind was full of the conversation he had just had with the Managing Director and the thought of something underhand going on right under Ron's nose was annoying him.

On walking back into the production office, Ron could hear Porkie on the phone.

"Can I speak to Mrs Thomas's little boy," he was saying. 'There he goes again', thought Ron. Although he quite liked Porkie, he thought Porkie was very unprofessional in his telephone manner and needed to be pulled for it. Some of the things he would say to certain customers was little short of being disgusting.

"Well, did you get the sack?" jeered Robby. Both Robby and Franco sat there with big grins on their faces. Ron glanced over to Porkie and he was also grinning as he fumbled with the telephone receiver stuck in his ear and carried on with his conversation with Mrs Thomas's little boy.

Ron just smiled back. He did not bother to answer, sat down at his desk and attempted to pick up where he had left off. His mind was full of what he had just learnt upstairs. He realised that everything in the office had now taken on a different image. He had in those few moments become suspicious of everything that was being said in the office around him. He was also looking forward to what he was going to tell Brenda that evening when he got home.

Tuesday evening was Ron's night for snooker at the club. He thought to himself as he reached the path that led to his front door, 'I wonder what's for dinner this evening'. Ben, who had been looking from the side gate, started to bark, letting Brenda know his master was home.

Brenda was in the kitchen. "Hi!" she called, believing that Ron would be starving. "It's lamb stew, are you hungry?"

"Fairly," was the reply. Ron, having removed his shoes and his coat, putting on his slippers and trying to push Ben away to stop him licking, said, "I've something to tell you. I saw Johnny from next door today, he's sort of asked us over for a drink one evening."

"What did you say?"

"Nothing. He said he would give us a knock one night. We'll see." Ron sat down and picked up the newspaper. Before he started to read he called to Brenda and said "But, I've something very interesting to tell you." He proceeded to shout out the conversation he had had with Bill Ross that afternoon as best as he could remember it and how the Managing Director had taken him into his confidence. As soon as Ron started to tell the story, Brenda stopped her chores in the kitchen and entered the living room. Ron, realising that he had captured her attention, began to dramatise the story, giving her no chance to butt in.

Brenda sat and listened and hung on every word that Ron said. She finally remarked, "He must have an awful lot of faith in you to take you into his confidence like that."

"Yes," said Ron, "And I've just had another thought. If old Johnny boy next door does invite us over for a drink one evening, I think it's better if nothing is said."

"Of course," Brenda answered indignantly. "I won't say a word."

"I know you won't, sweetheart," Ron answered, realising that he had just hurt her feelings, and carried on,

"What time are we going down the club?" He looked at his wife to see if she had forgiven him for the slight slip of the tongue as he gave old Ben a pat on the head.

"When you like," was the answer Ron received as Brenda left the room, smiling to show Ron that he was forgiven and thinking to herself that Ron was beginning to enjoy his job and it was nice to see him getting involved in work again.

Chapter 9

The next morning, it was drizzling slightly with rain. Ron decided that it wasn't too heavy and that he would walk to work as usual. He donned his coat, gave Brenda a kiss goodbye, gave old Ben a pat, told him to cheer up. (Ben always looked sad whenever Ron went out without him and set off towards the plant.) As he stepped it out on his way to work, he thought to himself, 'Good job I didn't have too much to drink last night, I've got to keep my wits about me today'.

On arriving at the office, he removed his coat. 'Isn't very wet,' he thought to himself as he put it on the clothes peg at the far end of the office. Robby's jacket was already hanging there, although there was no sign of him. Porkie was in too, his voice could be heard shouting above the noise of the machinery at some poor soul who had put a foot out of place or had made some small mistake.

Ron sat down at his desk, his mind very much aware of what went on yesterday and he said to himself, 'I mustn't become paranoid and imagine things. I must keep a clear head and only note the things that seem really suspicious.'

By eight-thirty, all four men were at their desks and, as usual, not much was said. It always took an hour or two for them to start communicating amongst one another at the beginning of the day, unless it was to do with work. Franco was chatting to Robby about a drawing in front of him and Porkie was rubbing the remains of the sleepy dust from his eyes.

The 'phone started to ring.

"Who's calling the golden shot?" Porkie said as he quickly picked up the handset which annoyed Ron. Apart from his piggish manner in snatching at the 'phone, what a terrible way to answer a professional telephone, went through Ron's mind.

"It's for you, Robby," he said. "Line one," switching it over to Robby's extension

"Thanks. Hello, good morning, Rob speaking, how can I help you?" Much better, Ron thought to himself, but the bright, crisp, clear, sound of Robby's voice was soon reduced to little more than a whisper. No one in the office took any notice but Ron made a mental note of it, making sure that he didn't let on that something could be amiss. Why would Robby lower the tone of his voice, Ron thought to himself. That must be worth mentioning to the boss.

As the morning progressed the work was beginning to pile in. Ron wondered to himself, whatever did Porkie do before he started there? He could not possibly keep up with the volume of work on his own. The others had told him that Porkie did all the ordering and job allocation before he had started there.

Twelve-thirty, lunch time. Before the big hand on the clock had reached the thirty minutes past position, Franco was out of the door and gone. He had obviously got a very important appointment. Robby was still at his desk, head down, involved in some complicated calculation. He wasn't such a clock-watcher as Franco and having started to work out the complicated quote from the drawing, was caught up in the intrigue of the calculation. The phone rang. Porkie snapped up the handset.

"Chinese take-away," he answered, jokingly, much to Ron's disgust. "Oh, right," he exclaimed. "Robby, it's for you, I think it's your old woman," he shouted across the office. "Line one."

"Cheers. Hello babe," he answered and carried on with what appeared to be a domestic conversation.

Ron tried to hear what was being said but was unable to understand as he could only hear half of the conversation and Robby wasn't being as loud as he normally was.

"Coming across for a coffee?" Porkie said to Ron.

"Yes, O.K.," he replied. They both left the office, letting Robby continue his apparently domestic chin-wag in peace.

Neither one spoke to the other as they walked across the shop floor heading for the staff room on the other side of the building. No point as conversation would have been difficult above the noise of the machinery. It was quite apparent that the shop floor staff had a wariness of Porkie, as they all paid more attention to what they were doing when they saw him approaching and behind his back, two of the more extrovert machine operators were saluting each other with big grins on their faces, probably done for Ron's benefit. They had obviously heard all, or some, of his army stories

On entering the staff room, Porkie put his hand deep into his pocket so as not to miss any of the small coins that could get stuck in the corners. Turning to Ron he said, "Tea ain't it mate, no sugar," as he sorted out the change from his pocket

"Yes, please," answered Ron. Porkie fed the drinks machine with the small change, which he was still sorting in the palm of his hand. The machine made the familiar noise as it dispensed the two teas. Porkie handed Ron his tea, then carefully put his own drink down on one of the empty tables and proceeded to unwrap a large egg and bacon roll, which he had brought with him from the production office. Standing with his back to the wall he started to eat his lunch and, as he took the first enormous bite, squirted most of the filling down his shirt and onto the floor.

"Oh shit!" he grunted and decided to sit at one of the tables, where he spread out the paper that had wrapped his roll, flattened it, in case any more of the valuable contents was lost, and continued to eat what was left of his lunch.

Ron finished his drink then threw the plastic cup into the half-full rubbish bin that stood at the door-way of the staff room. He then turned and nodded to Porkie as if to say 'I'll see you later.'

When Ron arrived back at the production office, he was surprised to find that Robby was still on the telephone. Ignoring Robby he sat down at his desk, and although the two of them were back to back, Ron made sure he heard every word that Robby uttered.

"Yes I know," Robby was saying. "I've told them twice that the television is at your mother's and has been there for nearly three weeks. I've told them straight that it's their fault, they were notified at least three weeks ago that the set was ready for collection. And I also told the silly tart that they won't get another penny and as far as we are concerned the set will stay there until they come and collect it." Robby was fiddling with his pencil, and doodling on a piece of scrap paper as he spoke. "Yes, yes, I know, all right, I'll phone you later. Bye, sweetheart. Bye."

Robby put down the handset, turned to Ron and said "What do you think? We've bought a new television and we are having hell's own job to get the rental company to come and pick up the old one. She's just had a reminder to say last month's bill hasn't been paid. She's doing her nut."

Ron just acknowledged Robby's comment, made a mental note and carried on with the backlog of work on his desk.

Robby went on with the story of the television, to Franco and Porkie in turn, during the afternoon. They both tried to show interest in his story but didn't show much enthusiasm.

Nothing much else happened until well into the afternoon, when Franco called Ron out of the office, onto the shop floor, so as to be out of earshot from the others in the production office. He was obviously very upset.

"Do you think it's right that he should speak to me like that?" he moaned. "I don't know who the hell he thinks he is."

"Who?"

"Robby. I'm not taking much more of it."

Ron had heard a slight ruckus at the desks of the two lads during the afternoon, but had put it down to a bit of horse play.

"I don't know," he replied, "but it's not worth getting uptight about, ignore it, you will be going home for the weekend soon. I bet when you come in on Monday you will have forgotten all about it."

"Yea, I suppose you're right. Thanks. You see, I can't talk to Porkie, that prat doesn't listen to a thing I say, the man's a bloody pig."

Ron had no idea that Franco was so against Porkie, but whatever the quarrel was between Robby and Franco, it was over at least until Monday. Franco returned to his desk, not looking at Robby, started to clear up his desk top, then sat in silence until it was time to be off for the weekend. He just tapped the keyboard of his computer occasionally to make out he was still working, for Porkie's benefit.

Ron pondered over what had gone on during the week and came to the conclusion that although probably of some significance, it was not really enough to worry the boss with. He decided to switch off mentally and go home to his mate, Brenda, for the weekend. Thinking to himself 'I wonder what next week will bring', he also wondered if the Boss was waiting for some form of contact from him, but decided that if he hadn't got anything concrete to report it was better to keep silent.

Chapter 10

Saturday was spent tidying the garden and sweeping up the fallen leaves, clearing the rubbish from the greenhouse and getting the flower pots emptied of their now-dead plants ready for the winter. Ron was thinking that next year he wouldn't have so much time to spend in his garden. This year was the first time that he had taken a keen interest in gardening and the new-found hobby was one of the few interests he could involve Brenda in. She had always loved her garden and was delighted that her Ron was finally helping to keep the place tidy.

After the midday meal Ron had taken Ben for a run on the common, and they were settling down for an afternoon of sport on the television, Ben laying at Ron's side, when the door bell rang.

"Who the hell's that? I'll go," he said as he pushed Ben out of the way. Ben followed him to the door tail wagging and stood behind him, waiting to see who would dare ring the door bell.

"Hello, mate, come in," Ron said to the chap standing in the doorway.

"No, I won't, thanks, I just popped over to ask if you and Brenda would like to come round this evening, for a drink or two. I'm having a friend in and I thought you might like to join us," said the very loud Johnny Gibbs, with a big smile on his face.

"Er, yes, I think so, what do you say love?" he called to

Brenda.

"Yes, that would be nice," was the answer as she also came to the door, pushing poor old Ben to one side so she could see who it was that Ron was talking to, knowing all the time that it could only be Johnny from next door.

The three of them stood in the door entrance and agreed that about eight o'clock would be ideal.

"Thank you, Johnny, see you later. Bye." Ron shut the door. "Well, there's a surprise, mate," Ron said. "Remember, keep your tongue between your teeth, just in case something is said about work. The less said the better."

"You don't have to worry about me. You're the one who is most likely to say something, especially if you have a drink," she answered, feeling slightly hurt.

Ben was left standing at the door, tail wagging in anticipation of someone else coming to the door but soon got fed up and went and laid at Ron's side.

Johnny's house was roughly the same size as Ron's. His garden, though roughly the same size, was all laid out to lawn and did look a bit of a mess with all the leaves scattered by the wind and not cleared up. Although this could not be seen in the dark as Brenda and Ron walked up the path in the light of Johnny's front door lamp. Ron rang on the door-bell and could see Johnny coming up the hall through the frosted door panel as he looked through the glass. They had been inside the house several times before, many years ago, when Johnny's ex-wife Susan was on the scene. In those days there had been quite a friendship between Susan and Brenda, and Ron had also done a spot of decorating in the house and had even helped with the garden.

"Hello, folks, in you come," was the greeting they received as Johnny opened the door. "Come through, I've somebody here that I think you know, Ron." As John led them into the lounge there, sitting on the sofa as if she was perfectly at home, was Jill, Bill Ross's secretary.

Ron was rather surprised and after the introductions Brenda, realising who it was, exclaimed "Oh, that Jill!"

fetching a smile from the others. Brenda thought to herself 'Ron was right, better keep the conversation off Precision Laser Ltd.', and continued to talk about any subject that did not include work at Lower Street.

The four of them passed a very pleasant evening and from the manner in which Johnny treated Jill, it was quite apparent that they were more than good friends. For the most part of the evening, Jill sat very close to Johnny and at one point was in fact holding his hand. Brenda noticed this and whether deliberately or not, made several references to Susan, which brought absolutely no response from Johnny at all. The house inside had changed considerably since the last time that Brenda had been in there and she thought that, although the furniture had changed, the home was missing the touch of a woman. Jill and Johnny made no attempt to talk of the firm but were quite content to talk about the new automobile parked in the garage. Ron, realised that the invitation for the evening must have been made to fulfil a promise and that Brenda and himself were really in the way of this apparent courting couple. They made short work of their drinks and thanked their hosts for a pleasant evening, made their excuses and left for an apparently early night.

After letting Ben out of the back door, the conversation between the two of them revolved around the relationship of the two in the house next door and what had been said during the evening. Indeed, they both wondered if Bill Ross was aware of the relationship.

"I hope he treats that girl a bit better that he treated Sue," Brenda remarked, just to ensure that Ron knew that she hadn't got a lot of time for Johnny Gibbs.

Chapter 11

On Monday afternoon the office was very busy as usual, nothing much had gone wrong, a few jobs had been slightly short but could have been attributed to bad setting up or bad workmanship. Fortunately, the two or three jobs that were short of material were able to be completed from the materials held in stock.

Ron, in trying to investigate the shortages from the wads of paper work that proved whether the material had arrived or not, quickly realised that the profit was being seriously eroded by having to keep drawing from that which should have been reserved for other jobs.

Robby picked up the handset of his telephone, dialled a number and proceeded, "Is that you, Smasher? Where are you?" Then a short pause as the person at the other end answered. "Good! As you come back, can you call in at the Corner Shop and get me a couple of bars of chocolate. I'm starving." He smiled at Franco, showing him his empty lunch box and carried on, " How long do reckon you'll be? Great."

The lorry arrived back in the yard. Dave, the driver entered the dispatch department. Robby shot out to meet him. They stood chatting and eating their chocolate, which was easily visible from the production office but out of earshot. Ron noticed this but as nothing could be heard, chose not to worry about it.

Dave, having put his paperwork in order from the day's

deliveries, said to Porkie, "What's on for tomorrow mate?"

"All local," snapped Porkie, "and if you get back in time, you can load for Lincoln on Wednesday, ready for an early start."

"Right."

'No love lost between those two', Ron thought to himself, as it was quite apparent that the conversation between the two of them was a bit strained.

Dave made a rude gesture, not unlike the victory sign, to Porkie behind his back as he left the office to go upstairs. Then Dave, Robby and Franco all began to laugh as Dave told the story of the time Porkie left his lunch on the back of Dave's lorry by mistake and it blew away as he was driving along the M25.

There was a good atmosphere between the driver and the two lads on the estimating desks. They always seemed to have a joke between themselves, although some of the jokes, Ron couldn't see the funny side of. Most of the time it was Porkie who was the subject of the jokes, but of course he never knew.

'Can you pop up and see me? Jill.' The note handed to Ron by Porkie as he went by, on his way to the dispatch department to organise the deliveries for the next day with Dave the driver.

Ron dropped what he was doing, went upstairs and Jill greeted him with a smile. "He wants a word," she said. "Tap and go in."

Ron knocked and entered.

Bill smiled and greeted him. "What's new mate?" Bill said.

Ron attempted to relay what he suspected and what was on his mind although most of it was probably not worth mentioning, he thought to himself. Bill sat and listened patiently. Ron was a bit longwinded in what he wanted to say but it was apparent to Bill that at least Ron's suspicions were feasible, although probably unlikely. The pair sat and thought and toyed with several ideas.

"Ron," said Bill, "leave it with me. I've got an idea. Come

and see me tomorrow afternoon and I'll let you know what I've decided to do. I'm not sure what I've got in mind is strictly legal." He paused for a moment still obviously thinking, his mind being miles away from the office then, realising that Ron was beginning to feel a little uncomfortable, enquired, "How is everything else down there? Are we getting plenty of orders in?" asked Bill, mainly to make Ron feel his trip to the boss's office had not been a waste of time.

" Yes, we are pretty busy," he answered. "Thanks." Ron knew the real reason for the question.

Chapter 12

Two-thirty had arrived and Ron made an excuse to go out of the office. He slipped upstairs and on the landing stood Bill Ross. When he saw Ron he grinned, beckoned him to the office, shut the door and they both sat.

"After what you said yesterday," Bill started, "I've taken some technical advice. I'm having a tape recording machine fitted to our telephone system and I hope to have it up and running by this evening," he said excitedly.

"Oh, good," but what he had just been told hadn't really sunk in.

"It will work like this," Bill went on. "It will be fitted to Robby's 'phone line at the distribution point where it comes into the building so nobody will know anything about it. Now, Robby's 'phone line is line number one and when any calls come through for Robby or Franco, they will be put through on line one by the receptionist and at night, the night service line for the whole factory has been converted so that line one is always the line in use. Line one will be in use every time the office goes home, so every conversation after hours and during the night shift and every time Robby uses his 'phone, we'll be able to monitor it. I don't think the receptionist understands what I'm doing, I've told her that Robby must use line one always because it's the line for quoting."

"Crafty," chipped in Ron.

"Yes, so what I want you to do is, every time there is a

call for Robby that originates through your office on your 'phone, is to pass it over to Robby, on line one, if that's possible. That way we will be able to monitor a good proportion of what is said by Robby and possibly the other one." Ron knew he meant Franco. By that reference to Franco, Ron realised that Bill Ross wasn't too keen on the lazy, little chap.

"O.K., we'll give it a go." Ron thought for a moment. "Yes, we'll see what happens." Bill explained it all to Ron once again to make sure he had grasped what he was trying to pull off.

Ron returned to his office, still deep in thought and was confronted with, "Getting friendly with the Boss, aren't we?" It came from Porkie in a very mocking tone.

"No, he wants me to deliver a message to Johnny Gibbs when I go home tonight," he answered, thinking quickly. "You know he only lives next door."

"What's the matter with his mobile then? I suppose he's got the bloody thing turned off again as usual, thinks he is above the rules that one."

Ron didn't answer. He was pleased to let the matter drop.

Working away Ron couldn't help smiling to himself. 'If they are at it, they are going to be in for a shock', he thought, 'especially if they are using the 'phones to pull off their little scam.' Dave the lorry driver came to Ron's desk.

"That prat, Porkie, doesn't know what he is talking about." he said. "The silly bastard might have known that the Lincoln Steel and the drops for Kings Lynn wouldn't be ready until Thursday. They've got another good day's cutting to do yet before that lot's finished and even then they'll be lucky."

"Oh!" Ron said looking up. "I suppose that means your early morning start has been put off."

"Yup, till Thursday. Upset my whole bloody week. Never mind, worse things happen at sea. Anyway, have you ever known Porkie to get anything right?" he said as he walked back to the dispatch area. Putting on his protective gloves as he walked away, he was smiling and had obviously been in conversation with Robby and Franco about something amusing.

Porkie, returned to the office, sat himself down and started sorting out the work for the night shift. Franco crept up beside Porkie and in a low voice, and as if he had just plucked up the courage, said, "Do you think it's possible that I could have four or five bits of three mil. mild steel, about a metre long by about sixty mil. wide? My dad's making me a pair of gates and I need the metal to fashion the hinges. I've seen plenty of three mil. in the second scrap skip."

Porkie's face was one of displeasure. He sighed and immediately picked up the handset of his telephone and in a dramatic manner 'phoned upstairs to Bill Ross's office and related the request. After a few minute's silence, Porkie, head nodding, said, "Right, O.K., I'll tell him, I will, thanks."

Replacing the handset on the phone, he faced Franco and said, "Yup, I think that'll be all right. Go and see Jimmy on number two machine and he will trim those bits of scrap for you, but make sure that you don't stop him working," he added, just to show his authority.

"Thanks." Franco turned and shot out of the door leading to the shop floor.

"Fastest he's moved all day," piped up Robby.

Yes, thought Ron, and looked up at Porkie and noticed from the expression on his face that he was having exactly the same thought.

"Pity he can't move as fast as that when he's quoting," Porkie shouted out, just to let the others see he had noticed Franco's movements.

After a few minutes had passed Franco returned, carrying four or five long pieces of metal.

"Bloody hell, what sort of gates are you making?" asked Porkie, referring to the size of the pieces of scrap. Everyone in the office turned to look.

"It's all right, isn't it?" said Franco very sheepishly.

Porkie, seeing that the man was embarrassed, replied,

"Yes, I suppose so. Go and put them in your car before the Boss sees them."

"Thanks," he answered and was gone.

Chapter 13

It certainly was getting colder. The heating had been turned up a notch or two in the offices and the fluorescent lighting was on all day.

Ron was very aware that the office was much brighter, or it seemed that way because outside was overcast and not throwing any daylight into the buildings. But the fluorescent lights were over-compensating, giving the whole office area an unnatural brightness.

There had been a whole series of 'phone conversations by Robby and Franco, most, from the sound of them, perfectly normal business calls. Ron was itching to know if the tape was in place and if, in fact, it worked.

Dave, the lorry driver, a likeable sort of chap, always pleasant, had taken to wearing a black woolly hat to keep out the cold. It made him look a bit silly. He always had a joke to tell and seemed to smile with his eyes. He had brought in a couple of compact discs and laid them on Robby's desk. Being curious, Ron interested in what the recordings were of, picked one up and started to read the label. "James Last Big Band," he read out loud.

Robby piped up, "Yes! I'm busting to hear them. I've only got records indoors and she's just bought me a compact disc player and I know the clarity is much better."

"That's nice," Ron remarked. "What, is it your birthday?"

"No! She's had a rise at work and she's treated me," replied Robby picking up the two discs and reading the covers again to himself.

Ron thought to himself, 'he's doing all right, only yesterday he told me he had just bought a new television set, now a new compact disc player, he must be doing something right.'

During the day Ron had made several 'phone calls and couldn't help wondering if his conversations were being recorded. He immediately thought of Brian's terrible telephone manner and smiled to himself. If the boss hears some of the things he says on the 'phone he's bound to pull him up for it.

Jill came into the office. "Where's Brian?" she asked. She never called him Porkie. Ron informed her that Porkie was either in dispatch or on the shop floor.

"Can you ask him to let me have the steel packing notes for this month?" Jill said out loud, then, leaning over Porkie's desk said to Ron in a whisper. "Can you pop up and have a word with you know who as soon as you can?" She looked at the others as she spoke to make sure that they couldn't hear. Having delivered her message she went back the way she came in.

Ron couldn't help noticing the smell of perfume as she left the office. He gathered up a handful of papers, not worrying what they were, pretended to put them in some form of order and, putting them in a folder under his arm, left the office.

As he arrived on the landing outside Bill's office, Jill remarked, "I'm sorry about that, but he wants to see you and he told me to be discreet. What's going on?"

"Nothing," Ron replied, knowing that Jill wasn't as daft as she looked. 'Not that she looked daft anyway', Ron thought to himself. He had always thought she was quite attractive.

Ron tapped on Bill's door. "Come," he heard and entered.

Bill's face was beaming. He said, "Listen to this," with a big smile, as Ron sat, leaning forward so as to hear every sound from the object that Bill had in front of him. On Bill's desk was a small tape recorder, black in colour, not much bigger than a packet of cigarettes.

Bill proceeded to turn the machine on. "The only problem is, you've got to monitor every conversation," said Bill as he switched the machine backwards and forwards, searching for the bit he wanted Ron to hear. Having found the part on the tape that he wanted Ron to hear, he said, "That's it, now listen to this."

Both men sat there quite still as the machine unfolded the conversation between a very annoyed man called Barry and their own little Franco from downstairs.

The conversation went:

"Barry, here, when am I going to get the rest of my bits, you promised me last Monday, you can't muck me about like this, I've got blokes standing about doing nothing waiting for these parts?"

"Yeah, I know, I'm sorry, I'm having trouble getting the stuff cut. Julian has let me down, he's been off for a couple of days. Now he's back, Porkie has put him on another machine, he's not on cutting at the moment."

"That's not my problem, you bloody well promised, you've had your money and I want my parts."

"All right, I'll see what I can do, but I can't promise".

"Listen, you little runt, I want those bits today. If you can't get them cut, then for goodness sake at least get me the material and I'll get the bloody things cut myself. I mean it! I'm pissed off with you."

Franco's voice quivered and quietly he answered, "All right, I'll get the material over to you by a quarter-past five this evening, if you can cut them yourself."

"Look's as though I'll have to, don't it? Next time, I won't part with my money first, and you had better not let me down."

They looked at each other as if in disbelief at what they had just heard. Sitting back in his seat Ron said "I thought it was Robby on the fiddle, not him."

Bill replied "There's more than just Franco in it, I'm sure, and now we know there is at least one operator involved, Julian! I'm surprised at him, I'm not worried about Franco, I was thinking of getting rid of him anyway, the lazy little so and so." And with a big smile on his face continued to say "We know Franco's customer has got his material don't we?"

Ron looked puzzled.

"Yes, the bits of scrap that he wanted for his gates yesterday afternoon, that's why I agreed to let him have them when Porkie Sharp 'phoned up. I'd just got this thing working then."

As the penny dropped, Ron gave out a little laugh and said "Yes, they were pretty big pieces for gate hinges. Now what?" asked Ron, as the two men sat looking at each other.

"Nothing," said Bill. "Leave everything as it is, carry on as though nothing has happened. Let them carry on, they'll hang themselves if we give them enough rope."

The two of them agreed. Ron went back to his office. He had butterflies in his stomach. He had trouble in believing what he had just heard and all of a sudden Franco looked a very different character to what he seemed before he had gone upstairs.

Julian, the operator involved, Ron didn't know, only by sight. He was in his early twenties and Ron had noticed him on occasions because he had a rather flash white sports car with personalised number plates. His car number was 'JUL1N'.

Ron remembered thinking when he first saw the car 'I bet that registration cost him a bob or two.' It was a number plate that you couldn't help noticing.

He was one of the more experienced operators and had come to Precision Laser from another laser cutting company. He had volunteered to work permanent nights and was quite friendly with Robby. They evidently had known each other prior to Julian starting at Precision Laser; they had worked together in a previous employment.

Ron had also noticed that on numerous occasions, Robby, Franco and Dave the lorry driver, had often congregated round Julian's machine before going home in the evenings, Julian usually working the night shift. So they would chat for a short while as the shifts swapped over.

Porkie sat working out the night shift schedules, talking to himself as he put the different job cards in different folders. Not an easy job, it required a good knowledge of what each individual operator was capable of and how long it took to run each job.

Ron felt the urge to take Porkie into his confidence. He wanted to tell Porkie what he knew, but knew he couldn't. 'Anyway', thought Ron, 'suppose he's involved.' He soon put the idea out of his head and continued to work whilst Porkie had a conversation with himself about the work load for the night shift.

"It doesn't look as if the jobs for Lincoln and the Norfolk run are going to be ready until Friday," Porkie muttered. "I've properly dropped a clanger with that one. Do us a favour, Ron," he continued. "Give these three a ring and tell them that we can't deliver 'til Friday." He handed Ron a card with three telephone numbers on it.

"Sure!" replied Ron and got on and did just that. Surprisingly not one of them complained of the late delivery, probably because he only spoke to the receptionists at the firms instead of the people who were waiting for the parts on the production shop floors.

Brenda sat with open mouth, stroking Ben, as Ron told her of the day's events. She couldn't believe that in the first place Ron's suspicions could possibly be correct and in the second place, that Mr Ross would have the telephones bugged.

"It true," Ron assured her.

She said, "Don't think I'm going to 'phone you. You don't think I'm going to have that Bill Ross listen to my conversation on the phone, do you?"

"Don't be daft. He's not interested in listening to you," Ron informed her and was rather annoyed to think that she thought her conversation was going to be of any interest to his boss. The two of them had a little laugh about what she had just said. Eventually the pair settled down for a night in front of the television, with old Ben sound asleep on the floor, on the mat in front of the fire.

Chapter 14

Next morning Ron was awake early. He hadn't slept particularly well. He took Ben for a short walk before breakfast, which normally he would not have had time for. With his sandwiches tucked under his arm he kissed Brenda on the cheek and made his way out of the door and headed towards the factory.

"Want a lift?" he heard, as Johnny Gibbs pulled up beside him in his company motor.

"Thanks," Ron said as he got in.

"You're about early, this morning," Ron commented.

"Yes. I have got to go in first, before I go to see Albion International. I reckon there's a big order there, if I can pull it off."

"Never see you in your new car, Johnny. Are you saving it?" making conversation Ron enquired.

"No, but I do use it most weekends, but you're right, I don't do many miles in it, anyway I'm teaching Jill to drive and for most of the time we use her car."

"Rather you than me mate, teaching a woman." They both smiled.

The short journey was soon over. Ron thanked Johnny and a little uneasily entered the office not knowing what the day was going to bring forth.

He sat at his desk, changed the date on the desk display in front of him to read Thursday, seventeenth, picked up his pen and chewed the end before he started to sort out his jobs for the day, waiting for the others to arrive.

The 'phone rang and as he picked it up he noticed that it was line one. "Oops," he said to himself, knowing full well that whatever he said was going to be recorded.

It was Robby's wife to say that Robby would be in, but he was having trouble starting the car, so he would be a bit late.

"O.K., I'll let Mr Sharp know," was Ron's reply. "Good-bye." Putting the 'phone down he thought to himself, 'I wonder what he's up to.'

"Mr Ross has asked if you will go with him to the garage to help him pick up his wife's car, Ron," said Porkie Sharp as he walked in from the direction of the executive offices. " I said it would be all right. He is waiting for you in the car park."

"What now?"

"Yup, get a move on, he's waiting."

Ron knew this could not be genuine and hurriedly donned his coat and went outside.

"Jump in." Ron did as he was told and waited for the explanation.

As they pulled out of the car park Bill said in a serious tone, "It's bigger than we thought, Ron. Listen to this." Bill pulled out from his inside pocket a cassette tape and proceeded to put it in the stereo unit of his Jaguar. Apart from the pure luxury of the car, the hi-fi system made what they were listening to absolutely clear and the voices were immediately recognisable. Firstly, Julian, talking to Robby.

"All right mate. I'm pissed off with Franco, he's buggering me about. He says he don't want those bits for his mate now, said he had to get 'em done elsewhere, but I know he's had the money for 'em, the shit bag. The little bastard caught me last time."

"Yeah, I know, I've had to tell him to get his act together. He is pissing me off, as well."

"It seems to me, Rob, that I'm taking all the risks and you lot are getting all the bloody cream. Last night, for example, I'd just finished cutting those four mil. bits and hiding the scrap in the boot of my car, when the old man came in. I felt sure he'd seen me, he came right over to me and stood at my machine. I shit myself but he hadn't seen me because he was ever so friendly, but, cor, I tell you, it was a bloody close call," said Julian.

"I bet! So those bits are done then?"

"Yeah!"

"Good, I'll get the delivery organised. That means we'll have the money by the weekend. I'll see Dave and we can do it the same as last time. I'll pop out in the lunch break and pick the money up. Right?"

"Yeah, but I'm going to want at least a hundred this time!"

"I know, I won't let you down, I gave you a ton last time. Don't forget I've got to give Dave some and Franco a few bob to keep him quiet."

Bill stopped the tape, and wound it forward.

Pulling off the road and into a pub car park, Bill stopped the car and looked at Ron and said, "After that they get involved in football." He added "We're not doing it for that but listen to this," as he wound the tape forward. "Now this will surprise you."

Julian's voice. "Can I speak to Tony, please?"

"Who's calling?" a woman answered.

"Julian." Then a pause as she obviously went to get Tony.

"Hello! mate, I intended to come round in the morning but never mind, I've got some good news for you."

"Yeah, what's that?"

"I think I've found some premises, on the Industrial Park, at Upminster, right size and almost on the M25."

"How much?"

"Twelve grand a year, which is about what we said. It's empty at the moment and I know the agent quite well. He tells me we are the only people at the moment who are interested in it. It looks as if it is ours for the asking. It really looks as if things might be starting to move."

"Great! I've got those drawings you gave to Robby and I've managed to get a copy of the customer mailing list from Dave the driver, he's been using it as a list of delivery addresses. I couldn't believe my luck when I found it in the lorry. Any news on the finance yet?"

"No! But I've got an appointment to see the manager of Cooper's on Monday at eleven."

"Good! Do you want me to come with you? I think I should."

" No! I don't think so, I can manage, unless you really want to come. I'll discuss it with you tomorrow when I come round. Don't forget I've still got to pay you for the ten mil. bits you did on Tuesday. Old Matt was chuffed with them because you did them so quickly for him."

There was a short silence as Bill turned off the volume on the tape. The two men looked at each other. Bill ejected the tape.

"Not much else on there, only gossip," he said.

"Who is this Tony?" Ron asked "I didn't recognise his voice."

" I'm not sure, but I'm pretty certain it's Tony Morrison. He used to work for us a couple of years ago. I sacked him when I found out he was spending more time looking after his own, rented properties than actually going out on the road looking for business. Johnny Gibbs does his job now."

They were parked in the car park of the Rose and Crown. Ron could see that Bill was upset. "Those greedy bastards are going to set up on their own," Bill said. "And they're going to undercut us and use our customers and finance it with the money they have nicked from us. Well, not if I've got anything to do with it. It's a matter for the police now. I'm going to get some advice," he went on as he started the engine and proceeded to drive back towards Lower Street. "We've got to get positive proof, Ron. You keep your ears to the ground and I'll keep you informed the best I can."

Arriving back at the works, Ron sat at his desk, his mind not on his job. He couldn't help worrying inwardly that things were going to get nasty, especially for the silly fools who were thinking they were getting away with it.

Ron wasn't aware that Robby had been told off by Porkie Sharp for being late. Ron had forgotten to pass the message on in the excitement of being taken for a ride by the Boss. He knew he should have apologised for forgetting, but thought it better to let things stay as they were. He did let Robby know that his wife had, in fact, 'phoned in. Robby wasn't very impressed.

Lunch-time arrived. Ron, feeling the need to get away from the atmosphere of the office, took a short walk out and around the car park. Several things worried him. One, was how the parts were being got out, and second, how was Julian getting the parts programmed to be cut. If Precision Laser had not done the jobs before, there would be nothing in the memory on the computers that controlled the machines for Julian to call up.

Ron thought, and soon realised that the Dave referred to in the taped telephone conversation, must have been the lorry driver and thinking on, remembered, Dave was off to Norfolk and Lincolnshire, first thing in the morning.

He decided that if Brenda didn't make too much fuss, he would get up early and follow the lorry. He realised that if Dave was taking the stuff out, he must, of necessity, deliver them either on the way out, or late when he was on his way back, because the customers must be fairly local, from what was said on the tapes.

During the afternoon, he made casual enquiries, so as not to be obvious, about the departure time of Dave the next morning and discovered that Dave was usually away by six o'clock.

Brenda wasn't happy about Ron's plan, but eventually agreed to go along with it. She made it quite clear that Ron was to keep well out of sight and out of harm's way.

Ron assured her that he had no intention of getting into any sort of conflict with any body. He did wonder if he should let Bill Ross know his plan, but decided against it in case it turned out to be just a wild goose chase. He knew that if he was right, Bill Ross would appreciate the information that could be gleaned and it would give Ron a lot of personal satisfaction if he could prove how they were getting the stuff out.

Chapter 15

Morning came, not too early for Ron as he had been awake for some time before Brenda brought his mug of tea. He said to Brenda "No breakfast for me, mate, I shouldn't be long. I'm only going to see which way he goes. I can't follow him very far." She was not a happy lady.

By five-thirty Ron was in place. He was parked about eighty yards from the plant gates, on the other side of the road. There was a slight mist and only the light from the street lamps was visible and they had a sort of haze around them. Ron knew he was in good time. He thought to himself that he should see Dave arrive and go and clock in. He sat there in the dark with no lights on and the radio on very low, and waited.

At five-forty, to Ron's surprise, the roller shutter began to open. Ron didn't hear it, it was the light from the inside of the factory shining out that attracted his attention. The lorry was being reversed out and as it reached the road, still going backwards, the roller door began to close, so he knew that someone inside had let Dave out.

Ron knew that the lorry must go in the direction of the town and had no reason to come his way. The lorry pulled away. Ron followed about a hundred yards behind. He had no lights on to start with, his heart was beginning to pump harder, he could feel his chest thumping.

'Right at the end of this road', Ron said to himself. 'Yes!' he said as it did. He knew that if it was to go straight on at the next junction, it would be going onto the bypass and up to the A13 and off for the day on a genuine run. But if it was to turn left, he would be heading towards town and even towards where the local industrial estates were. He slowed down as the lorry, some eight yards in front, approached the junction.

"Yes, yes, yes, there goes the left-hand indicator," Ron shouted to himself. "He's going somewhere first." Ron drove round the corner very slowly just in case the lorry had slowed down. It hadn't. He could see the tail-lights some distance in front, then for no apparent reason the lorry stopped. Ron could see the stop lights on, then off, and only the tail-lights stayed on. The lorry just sat there, nothing moved, not even any other traffic. Ron turned his lights off and parked as near to the kerb as he could, turned off his radio and waited.

'I wonder if he's seen me', he thought, his heart still going nineteen to the dozen. It seemed ages that he sat there when, suddenly, on came the reversing lights of the lorry and Ron could see the lorry moving backwards. Then the left hand indicator came on, and the vehicle moved forward and turned left into a side road.

Ron moved off and, realising it was a housing estate he was in, put his head lights on and as he approached the junction where the lorry had turned, slowed down slightly. He looked up the entrance where the lorry had turned. There to his amazement, was the lorry, on the right hand side of the road, outside a residential garage. The garage doors were open and in the beam of light shining out from the garage, were the figures, only just visible, of Dave the driver and Robby, both in conversation and completely unaware they had been seen.

Ron excitedly drove on through town, not really taking much notice of where he was going, he was in such a state of euphoria. He couldn't believe what had just happened and how easy it was to catch them. On arriving home, Brenda was waiting in the lounge, looking out of the window. She was looking worried in anticipation that something had gone wrong. When she saw Ron's car pull in the drive she tossed her head in the air and gave a little sigh of relief.

Ron, unable to hide his excitement, proceeded to tell her the events of the last thirty minutes.

" No," she said, "you've only been gone a few minutes," but she sat and listened to Ron's account of what had happened with disbelief and amazement.

"I'll make some more tea," she said. "Are you going to have some breakfast now?" she enquired.

"No," said Ron. "I'm far too excited to eat but I'd better phone Bill Ross and let him know what has happened."

"It's a bit early, he won't be up yet," she stated. "Sit and have a cup of tea, then give Ben a run, and by that time he should be up." Ron agreed. After the fuss Ben made when the lead was shown to him he settled down and walked quietly at Ron's side. Ron's thoughts were still following the lorry. He couldn't make out why it had stopped at the entrance of the road where Robby obviously lived.

It was just beginning to get a little lighter, the traffic was becoming thicker, as the town began to wake up. To save Brenda a trip, Ron bought a newspaper on his way back home. Just glancing at the headlines he thought same old rubbish. Just then, it hit him.

"Of course," he said to himself, "the lorry stopped to use the mobile phone, to wake Robby up, so they could unload the stolen parts into the garage. Yes, of course. He stopped to use the mobile phone." He felt relieved that he had solved the puzzle of why the lorry had stopped. It had been worrying him. He thought to himself that the phone company must have a record of the call but wondered if they, in fact, logged the times of calls.

On returning home, Brenda had made the breakfast. Ron really didn't want it but did his best to eat it. She let Ron know that she really didn't like what was going on. She also told Ron that he was lucky because, during the night, there had been a murder at Washington Road which is near the factory. She had heard it on the radio. Radio Essex was giving bulletins every half hour about a robbery that had gone terribly wrong. Ron was sympathetic but his mind was on the events of the morning.

Seven forty-five. Ron phoned Bill Ross. He explained in the greatest detail how he had followed Dave the driver and of the meeting between him and Robby. Bill listened with great interest to Ron's story and answered by saying that he appreciated every thing that Ron had done, but he didn't want Ron to go chasing about during the night and that the only way to get the proof they wanted was to have them followed and photographed, professionally, by a private investigator and that was indeed what he intended to do. Ron agreed and Brenda was extremely pleased about it.

When Ron arrived at work, he found it very difficult to treat the two boys in the office with the same courtesy as he had done previously, but managed to do so.

Bill Ross came into the production office about mid morning. He just asked, of Porkie Sharp, if things were going all right, he passed the time of day with Robby and Franco. It was obvious from the manner in which the staff answered him, that the staff had a lot of respect for their boss.

He spent a little time at Ron's desk and so as not to cause any suspicion, invited Ron to a coffee in the staff room. Fortunately, the staff room was empty, as it should have been at that time of day. As no-one was about, Bill started.

"I've been on to the police, and what do you think? I spoke to the desk sergeant at the local nick. They, in not so many words, told me that I should be able to control my staff." He went on, "I was damned annoyed. I have left my complaint with them but unfortunately, there has been a spate of robberies recently and all the CID are involved with them, plus there has been a murder, so they are going to contact me as soon as they possibly can."

"What, in the meantime, are we supposed to do, let them carry on thieving?" piped up Ron.

"Yes," Bill replied. "I want to make sure that we catch everyone involved, especially Julian and that Tony

Morrison. What they are planning could seriously affect this company." The two men just sipped their coffee. "I've got a firm of private eyes that are going to follow our lorries and they are going to log and photograph every move they make and I've told Steve Hawthorn, the night foreman, to keep his eyes on the scrap bins to see if any parts, unusual to us, are disposed of there, or if he sees any unrecognisable skeletons in there," said Bill. "Oh, and by the way, thanks for what you did last night and this morning."

"It was nothing," answered Ron.

Bill continued, "I hope you don't think that I don't trust you to follow the lorry, but I'm sure you will agree that it is much better to leave collecting the proof we need to the professionals."

"Of course. Brenda wasn't keen on my getting too involved anyway. She thinks I might come home with my nose spread across my face or something."

Ron finished his coffee and threw the plastic cup in the bin. Bill didn't drink all of his coffee, he wasn't too keen on the quality of the beverage that the vending machine delivered. He just put his half-full cup on one of the tables as he and Ron left the canteen.

They walked quietly back to the production office, neither speaking but both very deep in thought. They both felt the frustration building up inside them. Ron became more and more determined to catch the small group of cheats.

Chapter 16

Monday came. Ron had arrived at work first, as usual. Robby arrived next. He breezed into the office wearing a brand new leather jacket.

"What do you think of this?" he said.

Ron just looked. "Yes, nice," was Ron's reply but inwardly he was very bitter.

Franco and Porkie came in together and, as usual, the conversation was a little thin until the morning had progressed a bit. Robby seemed on top of the world and couldn't help mentioning his new leather jacket.

"It was only a hundred," he went on, much to Ron's disgust, and it was obvious that Porkie wasn't too happy about it either.

Porkie answered the phone in his usual manner. "Yes Sweetheart," he went on. "Hold on, I'll put you through to Robby. He's got a nice, new jacket," he said very sarcastically as he passed the phone over to Robby on line one.

Several things happened over the next couple of days which Ron attributed to the new found wealth of Robby and, to some extent, Franco. Dave the lorry driver was often in quiet conversations with the two lads.

Bill Ross summoned Ron upstairs. It didn't make any difference if anybody was suspicious of their meetings because Bill had got the evidence he needed and it was only a matter of time before the police could take over and start proceedings, although things still had to be kept very low key.

Bill, out of good manners, was keeping Ron up to date with events from the boss's angle. Ron hadn't realised the implications. Bill was explaining to Ron how he had advertised for more staff to cover the intended imminent loss of Robby and Franco. He went on to say that he was not worried about the driver as drivers are easy to replace. But if the lads were to see the advert for staff, it was to be made known that the company was expanding and that new staff were to be engaged for training. In the meantime, he said he had taken Johnny Gibbs into his confidence to prepare him so that it wouldn't be a shock if he was called in, from time to time, to help out with quoting in the production office. He told him that Robby and Franco were on their way out but he did not tell him the reason why.

Sure enough, Robby did see the advert and was tickled pink when he was told by Bill Ross that the expansion of the company included a promotion for him. He could not keep quiet about it, which upset Franco, so he had to be told that, whilst Robby was going to be the new plant production manager in the proposed new Midlands branch, Franco would be promoted to Senior Estimator and that it would obviously mean a pay rise for him.

The atmosphere in the office for a day or two was one of joviality as the two lads contemplated their good fortune. Ron couldn't help thinking that Robby was getting ready for an even bigger rip off, should he get his new fictitious position.

Bill told Ron that afternoon, he would be required to tell a police officer what he had witnessed when following the lorry. They were sitting in Bill's office browsing through the recordings waiting for the police to arrive, when one message from the recordings came over. Robby's voice.

"Yes, I'm all right, love. Yeah, I got it, now we can have a spend up and you'll never guess, the Boss has had me in the office this morning and offered me the chance to run the new plant in the Midlands. He says I can travel to start with and that he'll supply a car. I knew it was going to be our year."

The two men smiled at each other. Bill said, "I don't think we'll play that one to the police, do you, Ron?"

The police detective arrived, introduced himself as Detective Sergeant Frost.

"Not the Detective Sergeant Frost?" Bill said, all of them smiling. The detective must have heard that many times before.

After sitting and listening to the stories of the two men, the detective sat and thought and finally said, "What we've got here is clearly thieving, but I'm not sure that taped telephone conversations are admissible as evidence. Clearly the reports from the private detectives and their photographs are a good help in proving their guilt but I'll take the tapes and get them transcribed and I'll have a word with my Boss and see what he suggests. I'll give you a ring in the morning and let you know what way we are going to tackle it. We are going to need several officers to pull them all in together and keep them apart while we question them."

The three of them chatted while Bill got the tapes together. He had the parts of the tapes that had the evidence on them copied and the originals were given to the police. They finished the tea that Jill had brought them and agreed that the next day was not too long to wait, if the intended prosecution was to be clean and quick.

Chapter 17

The next morning, the police sergeant did 'phone and it was early. Bill thought that was a good sign. He said that he had had a chat to the Super and that the best way to proceed was to get a warrant to search Julian's house as it was suspected that he was taking paperwork and parts home. Then having got him, they could then pick up the other three all together. Bill agreed.

A date was set and it was mutually decided that the best time would be the afternoon of the following Tuesday. The plan was to arrest Julian at his home in the late morning and search his house. If that went all right, to arrest Robby and Franco around dinner time whilst Dave the lorry driver was out delivering. They were going to fetch four officers, two to do Robby and two to do Franco, so that the two lads couldn't talk to each other until they had been questioned in full. Then, when Dave came in from his drops, two of them would pop back and, as they put it, give him a tug.

Ron had been told of the plan by Bill and they both very excitedly chuckled together. They finally felt they were getting somewhere,

"Only a couple more days and they won't know what has hit them," said Bill. Ron wondered, if after it was all over, Bill would still take him into his confidence. Ron had got to like the involvement and, even more, he had got to like his boss.

Brenda was just as excited as Ron when he revealed the

plan for the next day. She was pleased it was coming to an end, although she knew Ron was secretly enjoying the intrigue and the involvement. Old Ben had never had so many walks, all because Ron wasn't sleeping properly. Because of the excitement he was waking early each morning and taking the dog for a walk.

One thing still worried Ron, however. Who was doing the programming for the machines to cut the parts? He thought to do the programming a computer was needed and the software, and that operation must be being carried out somewhere. 'Still, only one more day to go and then, with a little bit of luck, all will be revealed', he thought.

Bed wasn't very inviting. He knew he wouldn't sleep but for Brenda's sake he turned in to face what he knew was going to be a long night. During the night Ron kept turning over and over in his mind the conversations he had heard on the tapes. He was still having trouble coming to terms with the fact that those chaps could be working together to cheat their boss and pull the wool over the eyes of the others in the office. He wondered how long it had been going on and how much money they had actually thieved and another thought struck him. Who were all the customers?

At last the morning came. Ron got up early, as he knew he would. Brenda continued to fuss, Ben was taken for yet another walk. On returning with the morning paper, Ron tried his best to eat the breakfast that was prepared for him, to no avail. He kissed Brenda a fond goodbye and said, "Wish me luck." She did and, as Ron was walking down his path, Johnny Gibbs called out.

"Come on, Ron, I'm going your way." Ron got into Johnny's car and as they travelled, as Ron had expected, Johnny tried to pump him about what was going on at the office. Ron couldn't help it, he had to let on that he knew something but was strong enough not to say what it was. He did tell Johnny that by the end of the day he would be as wise as him, after all the Boss had told Johnny as much any way.

The office was empty, as usual for that time of day. Ron

had noticed Bill's Jaguar in the car park. On investigation, Ron found out that Bill was in the dispatch department and, on seeing Ron arrive, Bill called him over.

"Listen," said Bill. "Tell Porkie that I don't want Dave to go anywhere until at least eleven o'clock. We can't afford to have him back here when it happens."

"Oh, right! We had better make sure that he is kept busy. Porkie will soon keep him out of harm's way, he usually mucks him about and most times unintentionally."

The two lads arrived, both in high spirits and, unusual for them, they never stopped talking and joking. Porkie had come into the office and, as was his way, he tried to shut the lads up. It was too early in the morning for them to be so happy, he couldn't take it so early in the day.

The morning passed fairly uneventfully. Dave the driver was held up by sending him on a couple of local calls first, then by mid-morning he was allowed to load and get on his way.

At twelve-thirty both Robby and Franco went out to lunch. Tension was beginning to build up in Ron's stomach. He tried to stop looking at the clock. He knew that by now the police must have searched Julian's home.

Almost startling Ron, the office door from the executive block opened inwards into the production office.

"Ron, got a minute?" It was Bill, just poking his head round the door. He was smiling and beckoning Ron towards him, as he did so, looking round to make sure nobody else could see him. Ron got up and went out of the office into the corridor where Bill stood waiting for him.

"They've done Julian at his girlfriend's house," Bill said excitedly as Ron followed him upstairs. He carried on to tell Ron how, evidently, Julian had not lived with his mother for some time. "And guess what."

"Go on," Ron said impatiently.

"They have found a computer and a load of our programmes and a lot of the scrap from the parts they cut. They were in his garage. They are pretty sure that the computer is stolen because he says that he bought it off a bloke in a pub but can't remember his name or which pub it was."

"Oh great!" says Ron. "So that's how they were programming the parts they cut."

"And another thing, from the police records, both Dave and Robby have previous records but I don't know what for." Bill went on, "They certainly never put anything about that on their application forms, the sods." Then he proceeded to tell Ron that the police would be here at one o'clock and that Julian was singing his heart out and had named all three of the others and one other who had left the company, by the name of Steve Warlong.

Steve Warlong, had been one of the most experienced machine operators but was forced to leave Precision Laser Ltd because of a fight with Robby, earlier in the year, but that was before Ron had started with the company.

The lads returned from lunch, still in high spirits. Porkie Sharp came into the entrance of the office. Looking back over his shoulder he said, "I don't know what's going on, but there's a crowd of blokes just gone up to Bill's office." Nobody took any notice but Ron knew who they were.

Porkie caught Ron's eye and secretly said to Ron, "I've been told to take Robby over to the staff room for a coffee." In a whisper. "What's going on?"

Ron shook his head very slightly so as not to draw attention to himself. "Tell you in a minute," he said quietly.

Porkie invited Robby over to the staff room for a coffee as an excuse to get him out of the office and, no sooner had they left the room, when in walked Jill.

"Can you spare me a moment?" She said to Franco, who was still wondering why Robby had been invited for coffee without him. Then, with a big smile on his face, jumped up and followed Jill out of the door and up the stairs. 'This is it,' Ron thought, 'no chance of him doing any work at the moment.' He got up and looked out of the window to see if he could see any sign of any police cars in the car park. He couldn't. 'I expect they will be plain, unmarked cars, anyway,' he thought to himself.

Franco hadn't been gone long when he returned to the office, accompanied by two men, both in their early thirties, short hair cuts and both looked as though they could handle themselves. They, with the help of Franco, proceeded to go through the contents of Franco's desk, asking several times "Is this yours?" and "Is this yours?" Franco answering sometimes "yes" and sometimes "no". After a few minutes the taller of the two men said, "Right, is that all?" Franco assured him it was. They gathered up what was obviously Franco's own private property and headed towards the executive office block and as they went, Franco said to Ron, all red faced and a false smile on his face, "Cheerio, mate, I don't think they want me here." And they were gone.

A few minutes later Ron could see out of the window Franco and the two plainclothes policemen going through the contents of Franco's car and then the three men disappeared up the road in what could only have been an unmarked police car.

Porkie and Robby returned from the staff room, both men laughing. Porkie looked at Ron, as much to say, 'Is it safe to come in now?' Ron nodded knowingly at Porkie. They all sat at their desks. A few minutes passed and Robby noticed the contents of Franco's desk scattered all over the desk top and two of the empty drawers were left open. This puzzled him.

He turned to look at Ron and said, "Where's Franco boy gone? He's left a bloody mess over here." Ron didn't answer, he didn't have to.

A deep voice said, "Mr Robert Seals, I have a warrant here for your arrest. Mr William Ross here," pointing at Bill, "has instructed me to tell you that you are dismissed from this company's employment and that I am to help you clear your desk and escort you from the premises forthwith. You are charged with the theft from this company of unauthorised machined parts and that you have conspired with others to defraud this company of revenue." Bill Ross stood with the two plainclothes policemen at the side of Robby's desk.

Robby just stood there, the colour drained from his face. He hung his head, he didn't look at anybody. It was obvious that he was in a deep state of shock. The police officer continued to read Robby his rights. After a short while they cleared his desk in the same way as they had done Franco's. Then his car, in the same way and, just the same as Franco, drove off in the second unmarked police vehicle, Robby's silhouette being just visible, with his head hung low, in the back of the car, whilst the two police officers were in the front.

"Blimey! I expected him to make a fuss," commented Ron.

Porkie looked at Ron. "What in bloody hell was that all about?" he asked. Ron proceeded to fill Porkie in with the events of the last few weeks. He told Porkie every little detail. Porkie just sat there with his mouth open, listening. After Ron had nearly finished telling everything, Porkie butted in.

"Why the bloody hell didn't I get told about it? Who's the frigging Production Manager here?" Ron, as tactfully as he could, told how they didn't know who was involved and that he had been under strict orders from Bill Ross not to tell a soul.

"I thought you were getting bloody friendly with the boss," Porkie grunted. He wasn't very happy but soon lightened up when he thought of how the lads had always undermined him.

Ron, as tactfully as he could, said to Porkie, "Now you know, you had better go and see the boss, because Dave the lorry driver, is still out and he has got to be arrested yet."

With that small prompt, he was out of the room and up the stairs to see Bill Ross as fast as his legs would carry him. He obviously wanted to show that he was adding some input to the events of the day. Dave the driver was almost due back. Porkie had phoned him on the mobile phone with some pretence to establish what time he would be back in the yard. He was due at about three-thirty. The police had arrived and were waiting in the dispatch department, Porkie taking over, as if he had been in charge and overseeing the whole episode. Ron couldn't help smiling to himself.

The lorry pulled into the yard and Dave, after sorting his paperwork out, got down from the cab and walked to the door of the dispatch department. Opening the door, he was greeted by Porkie and the two policemen, the same two who had arrested Franco. As soon as Dave realised what was going on he let off a big sigh of relief and said, "I know, I've seen someone following me and taking photographs all week and I told Robby so. I've been expecting this."

The police went through the motions of searching the lorry but Dave rode to work on his push bike so, without more ado, he was taken away in much the same way as the others. Ron, realising that the lads who had been arrested were not going to be back for some time, with the permission of Porkie, made sure that Dave's bicycle was put in a safe place.

As the news spread around the factory, Porkie was busily telling everyone how he had single-handedly solved the mystery of the missing materials and that he had personally arrested the most dangerous of the criminals. Ron, overhearing, just smiled and was content to let Porkie Brian Sharp have his moment of glory.

The next day was Wednesday. Ron arrived at work. He couldn't help but notice that the cars owned by Robby and Franco and the bike belonging to Dave were still there. 'So they must still be in custody', he thought to himself. Porkie was already in and busy on the phone, telling all the regular customers what had gone on. Franco's desk had been cleaned out and Johnny Gibbs sat there, deeply involved in calculations and doing his best to cover the absence of the other two. Ron found it difficult to get down to work but as the morning went by, found the atmosphere in the office more acceptable and the work easier.

Bill Ross kept popping in and letting Ron and the others know little tit bits he was picking up from the police and several customers who had 'phoned in. Most of all, he wanted to let Ron know that the police were having trouble in identifying the computer that was picked up at Julian's.

By mid-morning, first Dave came to collect his bike, then a few minutes later, Franco turned up, then just as Franco was driving out of the car park, Robby turned up. It was quite apparent that neither one was talking to the other. They never showed any indication that they were upset but they obviously were.

Several days passed. Johnny Gibbs was involved in teaching a new chap that had just started the way to quote efficiently. His name was Michael, Mick for short, and he seemed to know what the job entailed and what it was all about, much to Porkie's annoyance. Porkie would make out that the job was a lot more complicated than it actually was. Ron was invited upstairs quite a few times to talk to the Boss. It seemed that the police were frustrated, although the evidence from the private investigators and the photographic evidence was all right, they were having trouble convincing the powers that be, to go ahead and prosecute. Two policemen were in regular contact with Bill Ross. They had been assigned to contact the firms that had been dealing with the thieves but the answers they were getting were "we thought that Robby was the governor," or that they had always paid cash and were waiting for receipts, and various other excuses all plausible but extremely unlikely.

Eventually Detective Sergeant Frost came to the firm. Ron was called to the office where, together with Bill Ross, he was given the official results of the police enquiry,

"Firstly," he said, "these may be of interest to you," and handed over about ten or twelve floppy, computer discs. "These are from the home of Julian's girlfriend. They have got to be returned to Julian as they are not stolen but whatever is on them may well be," he informed them, "so before we hand them back, they are yours to either copy or wipe clean of information relating to your company."

Bill arranged to have one of the computer programmers take the discs and copy them and without letting the policeman know secretly told the programmer that the discs must be wiped clean after they had been copied.

"Secondly," he went on, " the computer that was found at Julian's, we are going to have to hand back to him, because it is not on any list of stolen property. All four men have confessed now. They didn't to start with and only Franco engaged a solicitor, who, I think, told him to put his hands up." He cleared his throat, made himself comfortable and continued. "So, it has been decided by the powers that be that, on this occasion, the four of them will be officially cautioned and no other action will be taken."

Ron and Bill looked at each other in disbelief and before either could say anything the sergeant went on, "Julian has offered two hundred and fifty pounds and Franco has offered one hundred, probably on the advice of the solicitor as some form of recompense. I think you should take it." Then he apologised and said that although it was not a satisfactory result it was the best he could do. He then went into some lengthy speech about these guys being kept an eye on in the future, by the local boys in blue. All three sat in silence, Bill not knowing what to say. Ron could see the disappointment on his face. Just then the computer boffin returned with the blank discs.

"What was on them?" asked Bill.

"Not much except our quoting formula, as far as I can see," he said handing the discs back to the policeman and leaving the room. It was quite apparent that the Sergeant was embarrassed by the outcome of events. He made his excuses and left, taking the blank discs with him and apologising to Bill for not being able to help any further as his hands were tied, as he put it.

Ron and Bill sat and chatted for a short while, both men bitterly disappointed. Bill said he was going to 'phone Cooper's Finance Company, to make sure that the loan referred to in the taped telephone conversation, was not going be forthcoming, if he could.

"I'll tell you what, mate!" said Bill. "How about I buy you a drink on the way home tonight at the Hare and Hounds and we can put the world to rights and forget the whole bloody thing?"

"That will be nice, thanks."

"At least we've got them out of our factory and out of the system," said Bill.

"Yes, and I don't suppose they'll find another job too easily."

Ron arrived home and, telling Brenda the whole disappointing tale whilst eating his dinner said, "I'll tell you what, girl, if nothing else, I've made a good mate out of this and I'll tell you something else, if that had been money those sods were stealing, they would have been inside now. I reckon there is one rule for the big crooks and there is another rule for the small ones."

Chapter 18

Over the next few days the walk to work didn't have the same excitement or anticipation for Ron as in the last couple of weeks. The thought of them more or less getting away with their little scam was still stuck in Ron's mind. It had, however, made life in the office a little more difficult. Mick, the new boy, was settling in very nicely and had picked up extremely quickly the basic knowledge of quoting and even if he said it himself, Ron was beginning to do the daily tasks without having to think too much about what he was doing. Mick and Ron worked very well together but Mick was having trouble trying to come to grips with Porkie's way of working. Porkie always seemed to make an easy job much more difficult than it actually needed to be. Mick would often make little suggestions on how to do something quicker or easier and the answer would always be the same. 'When I was in the army we would do it so and so way.' Mick gave up and let Porkie carry on muddling.

Mick had been involved in precision grinding in his previous employment so the reading of technical drawings presented no problem to him. He was a young married man with a three-month old son. His wife didn't go to work, she was a housewife and mother full-time. Mick had a very dry sense of humour and outlook on life and could mimic Porkie with so much accuracy that, with your eyes shut, you couldn't tell which was which. Behind Porkie's back he would goose-step around the office, making an army-style salute and mimic the last order that Porkie had given, to everyone's amusement. He had an insatiable appetite for information about high powered automobiles and continued to talk about the latest and fastest models all the time. He was always turned out for work in a prim and proper manner, his trousers were always pressed and he took great care in his appearance at all times and before he touched any metal would put on protective gloves. And unlike Porkie's desk, his was always tidy, there was a place for everything and everything was always in its place.

Johnny Gibbs would pop in and out during the day just to check and see if Mick had any quotes that were causing him problems. In fact the four of them made an excellent team. Ron's friendship with Johnny didn't develop too fast, Ron was just a bit wary of him and Brenda was not keen, but nevertheless, Porkie, Mick, Ron and Johnny Gibbs were all able to rely on and trust each other in the world of Precision Laser Ltd. at least.

It had become a habit for Ron every evening, to call in at the Hare and Hounds on his way home for one or two pints, but no more than two pints, of Corton's Best Bitter. Brenda wasn't too keen on the idea at first but as Ron could do no wrong in her eyes, she soon adjusted and Ron's evening meal was put back an hour every evening. Most evenings Bill Ross would join Ron for a pint and a game of pool.

The pool table was always empty at that time of day. They had become quite good pals over the last few weeks and a spirit of competition on the pool table had developed between them. Ron calling on his snooker experience and Bill having his own billiards table at home, the two were evenly matched and the rivalry between them matched the same respect they held for one another in everyday life.

Bill often referred to the disappointment that he felt about those Scum, as he put it, getting off so lightly with their little scam. As a result of what happened, he had installed security cameras, inside and outside the premises at Lower Street, much to the disgust of the majority of the work force. The night shift in particular had put up some form of protest, but Bill had taken each and every one individually into his office and explained the situation. He asked them all for objections but because they were isolated from one another they all agreed that the precautions were necessary. When the cameras were first put into place they highlighted the length of tea and lunch breaks that were being taken by the mainly unsupervised part of the night shift, and when confronted with this information any argument they had was shot down in flames.

Porkie soon found out about the evening meetings between Ron and the Boss and lo and behold, before long, Porkie was making regular calls at the Hare and Hounds on his way home from work. Neither Ron nor Bill Ross had the slightest objection to Porkie joining them but it soon became apparent that he had a different outlook on life from the other two. He wasn't as generous and would expect a drink from the boss every time he walked in, which didn't really worry Bill, but Bill did have to tell him that the place to talk about work, was at work.

He found that Porkie's constant chats revolved around work and were spoiling his nightly challenge from Ron on the pool table and he, not ever likely to admit defeat, was getting behind with the running total of wins in the ongoing tournament.

A few evenings later they were playing pool as usual and the tension was building up as they came to a crucial part of a game. Bill was about to take a shot, he was snookered and if he missed hitting the yellow ball, he would certainly leave the game in Ron's favour. Ron was standing back, chuckling inside, knowing that if Bill missed, that would be the sixth game in a row in his favour. Bill was bending, eyeing up the best way to get out of the trap that he had been put in when "phone call, for Bill Ross," was shouted from the direction of the bar.

"Blast! Sorry, Ron, I won't be a minute." Bill went to the bar, picked up the handset of the small, counter-top, pay-phone. Ron could see him standing, leaning on the counter, motionless, just listening, then without saying anything, put the receiver down. He stood and thought for a moment, then turned to return to the pool table, Ron could see that he was either upset or angry, his face was white and his expression was one of tense thought.

"Trouble?" said Ron. He just got down and took his shot and missed by a long way.

"Sorry, Ron, that spoilt the game, you win," he said with a false smile. "Do you mind if I just sit and finish my drink?"

Ron sat next to him. They both took a mouthful of beer then Bill, as if he knew that Ron was going to ask what the matter was, said, "That call I had … I don't know who it was but it was a woman's voice and she said 'Mr Ross, I know you are in there because your Jag is outside and usually is at this time of night, be very careful because the police in Chadwell don't like people who drink and drive, you have been warned!' I can't think who it can possibly be. Isn't it bloody annoying?"

"Christ, who on earth would make a call like that?"

"I don't know, but whoever it was wasn't joking. I never have more than two anyway, so I'm not going to give them the satisfaction of letting them see I took any notice of it. Come on, one more game and this time, no interruptions and we'll see if you can make it seven in a row."

Chapter 19

The next morning Ron walked as was usual, thinking to himself that the blokes in the office would be bound to ask who won last night and that he would make small of the fact that the scores were now eight in a row for himself. Mick was already in and, smiling as he went into the production office, Ron said, "Morning."

But instead of the usual answer he got, "Have you seen what someone has done to the windows in the executive office block?"

"No what?"

"Go and have a look."

Ron went through to the main offices and was met by Bill. "Seen this lot, mate? I was called out in the night, look at the bloody mess." Every window on the ground floor was smashed, including the small vents at the top of the main windows and large lumps of broken concrete lay scattered where they had fallen after being thrown.

"Good heavens, do you know who did it?"

"No, it's all on film and the police have viewed the video but what with it being dark and them having taken the precaution of covering their faces, it's not possible to recognise any one except that they were young and a couple of them had bicycles, the little sods."

"You don't think its anything to do with Robby, do you? He's got a couple of young sons and they come from a rough part of town, seems a bit of a coincidence?"

"I don't know, but somebody has certainly got it in for me but I won't let them see I'm annoyed. I'll just get it all repaired and act as though nothing has happened and, just to be on the safe side, I'll only drink orange tonight when I see you at the Hare and Hounds."

"Yes, that would be wise."

"Ron, do me a favour, ask Porkie to organise some staff to clear this lot up and I'll see you this evening."

"O.K."

The broken glass was cleared away by two of the machine operators who seemed to make the job last a long time. It was a change from the monotony of standing at a bending machine and certainly a lot less effort. The glazing company worked well into the night to replace all the broken windows and indeed a couple of the window frames needed emergency treatment, such was the viciousness of the attack. Ron secretly admired the way in which Bill Ross was handling the situation. Although he must have been fuming inside, he showed no sign of being upset and indeed made several jokes speculating as to who could be responsible for the cowardly act.

The police returned the video tape after studying it for some time without any further information as to who they thought could have done it and agreed to patrol the area at more regular intervals during the late night and early hours of the morning. After inspecting the whole of the premises to ascertain why the night shift had heard nothing, they agreed that the machinery noise and the location of the main office block made it difficult for anyone inside the factory to hear what was going on in the executive car park area.

Two hundred yards further along Lower Street was a firm that made rubber mouldings for use in the car industry, Chadwell Components Ltd. They also ran a night shift and Bill Ross had, on the odd occasion, played golf with the plant manager, Jeff Morton. Jeff was one of Bill's mates from way back when Bill was a service engineer for International Laser Cutters Ltd. and Jeff was working as a van salesman for a motor factor company.

Being a nosy sort of chap he 'phoned Bill to find out what was going on with all the damage. After having been put in the picture by Bill, he agreed to get his night security staff to keep an eye on things at Precision Laser from a distance. Especially the executive car park area in case there was a recurrence of the event and made arrangements for the gateman at Chadwell Components to telephone the night shift at Precision Laser if anyone was seen lurking about.

Chapter 20

Early December and seats for fifty people had been booked at Felmore's Country Club for the Annual Christmas Party by Jill, on the instructions of Bill Ross. Bill had invited several of his own personal guests and staff and workers made up the rest accompanied by their wives or girlfriends. The response from the shop floor was never great, as Bill paid for the tickets for all the work force but, as usual, made it a rule that all partners were to be paid for by their spouses. The date was set for the second Friday in December and, as the day drew near, arrangements were beginning to be made about transport to and from the smart venue.

Ron, of course, had never been to one of these do's before and Brenda was looking forward to it, having spent a fortune, as Ron put it, on a frock. The frock was, of course, a very elegant inexpensive cocktail dress that flattered Brenda's figure and made her stand out as one of the beauties of the evening. Ron knew this and was very proud to have Brenda on his arm when he walked into the hallway of Felmore's Country Club.

Bill Ross was dressed in an immaculate evening suit, obviously very expensive, with heavily embroidered lapels of an unusual colour of blue, almost black. Next to him stood his wife, Marion, at the entrance of the hallway to greet everybody as they arrived and make sure everyone had a drink. Not everybody was wearing evening dress but all Bill's personal guests were and most of the staff. The shop floor lads and their partners were, in no way, made to feel inferior because of the fact they were not in evening dress.

Bill greeted everyone the same way and did his best to make everyone feel that they were the most important person in the room. Ron arrived with Brenda, a little late. Bill and Brenda had never met, nor had Ron and Bill's wife Marion. When Ron introduced Brenda to Bill, Bill made such a fuss of her that whatever happened the rest of the evening, Brenda was going to feel on top of the world.

Ron, after being introduced to Marion, took her to the bar, where the drinks already poured, were lined up on the counter ready and waiting. Marion, a woman just a little older than Bill, extremely dignified and very glamorous, warmed to Ron's simple outlook on life and his straightforward approach to everything he wanted to say. They immediately hit it off as friends.

After a good deal of pre-dinner mingling and pre-dinner drinking, the four of them sat together, and although the evening was to mark the celebration of the festive season, with workmates and invited guests, the four might just as well been on their own.

The wine flowed freely and the meal was almost over. The party was getting noisier and nearly everyone was laughing at things which, normally would only have brought a smile. Ron and Bill sat in their stupid paper hats as did everyone else, except Marion and Brenda who, having been complimented on their appearance, would not disturb their hair. During the meal the music was sufficiently low, so as to be able to speak in reasonable comfort. Now the eating was over, the band, intent in getting everyone on the floor dancing, had put up the volume to such a level that both Bill and Ron took refuge in the bar area. The two men sat and, as usual, enjoyed each other's company. Their wives, entertaining each other, danced with the group on the dance floor, mainly women. During their time at the bar they were visited by Johnny

Gibbs, who didn't exactly make himself a nuisance but kept trying to bend Ron's ear back about who was the best firm in East Anglia and the Home Counties to buy sheet metal from. Ron agreed with everything he said, knowing he was talking to about two bottles of red dinner wine. Then Porkie arrived in a similar state and, in turn, several of the other work force, all quite intoxicated and all talking complete rubbish.

As the evening developed, enjoyable though it was, it became apparent that Jill, who had arrived with Johnny Gibbs, wasn't as happy as she should have been. She kept looking daggers at the man who, to all intents and purposes, was her partner for the evening. Johnny was ignoring her. Although bad manners, he was flitting from group to group trying to get the party going and being very generous, buying rounds of drinks. Brian, as was his way, never said no to anything that was offered to him and his small oriental wife was keeping an eye on what he was drinking. After a short time had passed, Johnny had run out of steam and, the worse for drink, sat at the opposite end of the bar from where Ron and Bill had sat.

He was intent on talking to the young lady behind the bar who was really too busy to talk to anyone and wasn't listening to him anyway. He wasn't making himself a nuisance but he certainly was not impressing Jill. She tolerated the embarrassment for some time before making her way to the table where Brenda and Marion sat with their husbands. She didn't seem upset but, relying on the atmosphere to hide her intentions and being slightly inebriated, immediately started to flirt outrageously with first Bill and then Ron. Although the two men didn't mind or take much notice, the two wives did notice and, realising what she was up to, put her firmly in her place, not nastily, but with just the right amount of pressure that the occasion required so as not to upset the evening. Bill knew from the look on the girls' faces that they were not amused. To save any further embarrassment, Bill called Johnny away from the bar. What was said may never be known, but Johnny and Jill soon left and started the beginning of the end of what had turned out to be a very pleasant evening.

When they arrived home Brenda sighed, then yawned repeatedly. She had enjoyed the evening so much she could not stop talking about her new-found friends and what a lovely couple they were and how Marion was such a lovely person.

"Oh, and by the way, Marion isn't keen on Bill going in the Hare and Hounds every night and tomorrow she is going to ... zzz zzz zzz ..." Two minutes later she was sound asleep.

Ron gave her a little peck on the cheek, put the light out and said, "Night, sweetheart, God bless." Ron had not seen Brenda so relaxed or so intoxicated for many years. He was delighted she had enjoyed herself and that she had met and liked Bill and his wife.

Chapter 21

After the weekend the office was made more aware of the festive atmosphere. A feeble attempt at putting some Christmas decorations up had been made by Mick and Ron. 'Not many,' as they were told by Porkie, 'this is a place of work, not a Father Christmas Grotto'.

Four or five Christmas cards had been received and stuck on the wall with Blutack. Steel stockholders and suppliers' representatives were calling regularly and Brian, showing them that he was in charge, would take them to the staff room, in turn, to buy them coffee. They, in turn were leaving the usual Christmas goodies, large glossy calendars, desk top clocks showing in large print the phone number to call when their particular product was needed and, of course, several bottles of famous-brand Scotch Whisky.

Porkie would smile whenever he received a bottle and made sure it was put safely away in the large bottom drawer of his desk which was always kept locked.

Johnny Gibbs was a far less frequent visitor of late but in the run up to Christmas he was not wasting his time going out visiting prospective customers and was spending more and more time in the office. He had not mentioned the incident at the Christmas party but before mid-morning on the Monday after the party a large bouquet of flowers had arrived for Jill with a sealed card and everybody assumed that Johnny must have sent it. He had been very moody over the last couple of weeks and had asked for some time off work to sort out a problem of a domestic nature which, by now, everyone assumed had been sorted.

Brenda told Ron that a For Sale sign had been erected in Johnny's front garden and that she, being nosy, had 'phoned the Estate Agent to enquire how much the property was on the market for. The price that it was up for was way over what the property was worth and Brenda's comment was, that he didn't really want to sell it. Ron agreed, but as he was getting on well with him at work, was prepared to give him the benefit of the doubt.

Several rush jobs for the first of January were needed before the Christmas shutdown as the whole place closed from Christmas Eve when usually everybody let their hair down until the second of January. They would have to be fabricated and delivered before the shutdown. Johnny, being at a loose end, became involved in the processing of these orders. He took the opportunity of enlarging on his theory that the best steel to buy was the steel that was supplied by Jonathan Tornton Ltd., of Romford, because they could deliver three times a week and that they would, if necessary, put a special delivery on, for the firm's benefit.

"Great," replied Ron, "but so will two or three of the others. There isn't a supplier that we deal with that won't do a special drop for us."

"Yes I know, but you've got to be careful. In my capacity as Quality Controller, I see all the bad jobs that have gone out from here and I can honestly say that I've never had trouble with the quality of steel from Tornton's. At one time or another, most of the others have given trouble, especially in bending, some of the cheaper imported steels crack during bending, although the material certifications show that they are up to standard. Tornton's only use the best British steel and their de-coiling plant is one of the most up to date in the country."

"Oh, right, well, I guess you know best," answered Ron.

Porkie was sitting opposite and heard the conversation and as soon as Johnny left the room he looked out of the door through which Johnny had just made his exit and, making sure he was out of earshot, said, "That's the biggest load of bullshit I have ever heard. What a plonker, take no bloody notice of him, and besides, Tornton's don't have a de-coiling plant, they buy all their steel in, already de-coiled. I've been to their place on two occasions and I've never seen a de-coiling plant there."

Ron sat and felt completely confused. It was noted that Porkie was under the impression that Johnny, in his capacity as Quality Control Manager, was superior to Porkie, but both Mick and Ron knew that this was not the case, although Johnny was by far superior in his manners and basic common sense. Porkie let himself down by his crude remarks and his lies to get himself out of trouble when he made a mistake. He made himself look small and stupid but he didn't realise it. He had a bad habit of not admitting he was wrong if he had made a mistake but would always try to lie his way out of the problem.

That evening, as normal, Ron was joined by Bill Ross at the Hare and Hounds and, because of the time of year, it was getting harder to have an uninterrupted game on the pool table. The evening trade for the public house was starting earlier and the pool table was in more or less constant use. So the two friends would sit and chat for a half an hour, unless they were lucky enough to be there first in, when they could have one quick game. During the conversation it came to light that the freebies, the bottles of drink that were being collected by Porkie, were not known about by Bill and he was quite surprised to hear that Porkie was making a collection of them.

"I'm surprised at Porkie. Those gifts are for all the staff who are involved in ordering material," Bill said. "Leave it with me, I'll have a word with him. I think he is being greedy."

"I don't want to cause any trouble, I didn't mention it to get him into trouble."

"No, I know, but I think he's being bloody greedy and it's got to stop."

Just then a familiar voice could be heard rather loudly at

the bar.

"That sounds like Robby," said Ron. They both looked in the direction of the bar. It was and, from the look of him, he had been drinking. His hair was all roughed up and he was slightly slurring his words.

"Leave this to me," said Ron, as he got up and made his way towards the bar area where Robby was standing, thinking that there might be some trouble.

"Hello Robby, how are you?"

Robby turned to face Ron and he must have seen Bill Ross and said, in a loud vindictive tone, "How am I? Well, I'll tell you how I am, I'm skint, my old woman has pissed off with the kids, I'm working as a fork lift driver for peanuts and if I don't make a payment on my mortgage, they're going to start repossession proceedings against me. Apart from that, I'm on top of the bloody world, so don't ask. I suppose you blokes at Precision are laughing your cocks off."

"No, we are not and I'm sorry I asked."

By this time Bill Ross, hearing the comments from Robby, had walked over and stood next to Ron and facing Robby said, "Hello, I hope you don't blame me for your situation, Robby?"

Robby looked hard at Bill, thought for a minute and replied, "No, it's my own stupid fault. I had a good job with you and I blew it and it takes a lot of guts for me to say this, Mr Ross, but I'm truly sorry for what happened." Robby took another mouthful of beer and said, "I've thought about what happened, you annoyed me when you made out I was going to be promoted, you made me look stupid in front of my family. I know I deserved it, so you won't get any more silly phone calls and I'm sorry I wound my kids up so they damaged your factory. There I've said it. I wasn't going to, but it's been playing on my mind. I feel a bit better now that I have told you but, rest assured, I will never admit to it if I'm questioned about it again. See you. Good bye." He put his half-full pint of beer on the bar, nodded at both men and walked straight out of the bar and was gone.

"Well." said Bill.

"I reckon that's the first step to asking for his job back," Ron grinned.

"No chance," acknowledged Bill.

The two of them chatted about what had just happened for a few minutes. At least the mystery of the 'phone call to the pub about drinking and driving was cleared up and the answer to who damaged the factory was now also explained.

"What are you going to do about it?" asked Ron.

"Nothing, what would be the point? No chance of getting any compensation there, you can't get blood out of a stone and even if you could, what good would it do us? None!"

They both agreed, drank up, bid each other farewell and left for home.

The next day Ron, feeling slightly awkward about what he had said to Bill in the pub the previous evening about the free bottles of booze, enquiringly asked of Porkie, "What's happening to all the booze you've collected then, mate? Are we having a share out?"

Porkie's face was firm and his mouth was tight. He looked indignantly at Ron and said, "Share out? As far as I'm concerned, it's been shared out." Then realising what he had said and, unusually for him, showed a little embarrassment. He then made an excuse, got up and went out onto the shop floor.

Ron sat and, although he felt a bit awkward, was now very pleased that he had mentioned it to Bill the night before at the Hare and Hounds. Mick, overhearing the conversation chipped in, "What was all that about?"

When Ron told him and that he had told the boss the night before, the two men chuckled together, knowing that poor old Porkie Brian was in for a lesson on being greedy and selfish.

Bill Ross was out for the morning and Jill had been down twice to see if anyone knew where he was. He had 'phoned in earlier but hadn't let anyone know where he was and what time he would be in. Jill was distinctly below her usual happy self. She was pale-faced and she certainly wasn't paying the same attention to her personal appearance, not that she was untidy but normally she would cause most of the staff to turn and take another look or call for some remark a bit near the knuckle to be implied. But for the last couple of days everything seemed too much trouble for her. Porkie wasn't her favourite person, she could not stand his smarmy attitude or his crude innuendoes and would normally ignore them, and him, but today she made it quite clear that Porkie should stop his sexist remarks. What he had said to her could only be guessed but, as usual, his thick skin made anything she said go right over his head and he would just smile, looking for support from others in the office.

When Bill arrived in the early afternoon, just after the lunchtime break, he was dropped at the entrance to the factory, in the executive car park by Jeff Morton, the plant manager of Chadwell Components. It was quite obvious that he had been mixing pleasure with business somewhere. His face was rosy, his top button on his shirt was undone and his gait was that of a sailor in a heavy storm aboard ship. He came straight into the production office, sat in Porkie's chair, Porkie being on the shop floor somewhere, and with a big stupid grin on his face said, "Hello, Ronny boy, how are you? What's the score now? I think you're about two in front but not for long, I'm going to have you tonight, I'm beginning to get the measure of you, you are not as good at pool as you think you are."

Ron smiled, he wasn't used to seeing his boss behave in this way.

"We'll see," he answered. " It'll depend if we can get on the table or not."

"Oh! by the way, where's Porkie? I want to see him. I think he owes us a bottle or two. Mick, do us a favour go and tell Porkie I want to see him."

Mick, smiling to himself, went to call Porkie. He wasn't a great lover of Porkie and couldn't wait to hear what the boss was going to say to him.

Mick and Porkie entered the production office. Porkie was carrying two or three job cards and laid them on his desk, on top of the pile of other cards that were already there and stood at the side of his own desk, half expecting Bill to stand up and give him back his seat.

" Brian," Bill started. "It's come to my attention that at least twenty bottles of Christmas cheer have been donated to our company, as a gesture of thanks for the patronage we have given our suppliers during the past year." He spoke very slowly and deliberately. "Is that correct?"

"No, Bill, about a dozen." Porkie's face was beginning to colour up.

"Where are they?"

"There's two in my desk."

"Where's the rest?"

"Um," Porkie looked round the office, he couldn't hide his embarrassment and in a very low voice said, "I took them home."

"Well, I suggest, that you bloody well bring them back. What gives you the right to think they are your exclusive property? They are for everybody who has anything to do with ordering material and services and I think you are being bloody selfish."

Porkie tried to front it out by saying, "O.K., I'll fetch them in tomorrow. While we are chatting, can I have a word about the gas pressure on number three machine?"

Bill didn't answer. He just got up and walked away from Porkie's desk, winking to Ron without anyone noticing. He headed for the staff room, no doubt to get a coffee before he could make an attempt to get his head round any work.

Ron and Mick kept their heads down, making out it was of no consequence to them. Both were smiling inwardly, they both knew what they had just witnessed was out of character for their boss. He had never intentionally set out to belittle anyone before, especially in public. Both men waited patiently for Porkie to leave the office and when he did, they turned to face each other and simultaneously burst out laughing.

Ron went to the pub as usual on the way home and was not a bit surprised that Bill didn't turn up. He thought to himself, 'I hope Marion doesn't think I had anything to do with getting Bill in that state', but at least he didn't have his car with him.

The following day Porkie was in early. He secretly took his store of fourteen and one half-full bottle of various spirits, up to Bill's office. He was pleased that Bill wasn't there but much to his displeasure Jill, having been already instructed by Bill, shared them out between the production office and the girls responsible for the paperwork side, making sure that Porkie's share included the bottle that had been started. He must have been fuming inside for making himself look so greedy, but his thick skin hid any embarrassment he had and the subject was never mentioned to his face again, although behind his back most of the factory knew about it.

Chapter 22

With Christmas and New Year out of the way, the weather frosty and bitterly cold, Ron was still walking to work. The daylight hours were lengthening although Ron's walk to and from work was still in the dark. He still enjoyed the time on his own to get his mind into gear for the day ahead. The cold didn't worry Ron, he was kept warm by the smart heavy-lined, blue, waxed coat that Brenda had given him for Christmas and over the shut down period, he and Ben had made good use of it on their regular walks. Ben still showing his years, was much more comfortable with this climate than he had been in the heat of summer.

The end of January heralded the end of the financial year at Precision Laser. Everyone was involved in stocktaking, in separating free issue materials from that which was owned by the company, in checking what completed jobs were to be delivered before the end of the month and numerous other tasks. A team of auditors spent several days at Lower Street, asking questions and making sure the figures that were being collated were as accurate as they possibly could be.

Ron still met Bill and most evenings Porkie as well, at the Hare and Hounds on the way home. The pool table was not in use quite so regularly as it had been before the Christmas break and the rivalry between Ron and Bill had rekindled itself. One evening during the Christmas shutdown Ron, with his Brenda, had spent a lovely evening at Marion and

Bill's home, where the two men played snooker into the early hours of the morning. Even on Bill's own table the two of them were very evenly matched. Bill had given Ron a top class snooker cue as a present for Christmas, which Ron treasured, but would really rub it in when he beat Bill with it.

Two meetings were called by Bill Ross in the staff room at the beginning of each shift, one meeting for the day shift and one for the night shift. Bill, equipped with the results of the outcome of the financial year end stocktake, proceeded to explain how, unless more care was taken with materials and setting up machines for test cuts, it was going to be impossible to make a profit. Most of what was said went over the heads of the machine operators but when Bill explained that nearly fifty per cent of every pound was being spent on material and that the company could not exist with this much being spent on material, it did start to sink in. Even allowing for the material that had been stolen earlier in the financial year by Robby and his mates, during the fiddle that they ran, which really was an unknown quantity, the firm couldn't make a profit.

Ron went up to see Bill in his office. He could not throw any light on why the steel bills were so high but felt he had to say something, as part of his job was to get the best price for materials and only order enough for each job. As he approached Jill's desk she was very down in the mouth and Ron tried to pull her leg but she was having none of it.

"He's on his own, you can go in," she said.

"Come in, mate, what can I do for you?"

"I don't know, I feel I must say something," Ron said, sitting down. "I'm not happy about the steel situation. I've given it a lot of thought and if what you said is correct, I think we've still got a problem. I only ever order enough steel for a specific job, except for the monthly stock order and very rarely are we short now."

"I know, I've checked, but something is going wrong. Last month, for example, we turned over just under two hundred thousand and our steel bill came to seventy four thousand. Ron, we can't go on like that. I've had Jill checking every packing note and invoice that has come in over the last two months, I've asked the audit team to have another look. If we can't get to the bottom of it we will have to look at the quoting system but I know that can't be wrong, we've used the same formula for years."

"Bill, the only thing to do is to pick a job and monitor it at every stage through the production and monitor the material, the time the job takes, and vet every piece of paper work connected with that job. Right down to the delivery notes when it leaves the premises."

Bill looked up at Ron. "You're not just a pretty face, are you, mate?" With a little smile he went on, "Yes, good idea, Ron. You pick a job, a nice meaty one, I'll pull the job card at every stage and we'll try it. Give me a ring when you've decided which one." Bill hadn't thought of doing that.

Ron said straight away, "We've just had the repeat order in from Watkin's, it normally takes about thirty five sheets of three by one and a half, six mil.. I haven't ordered it yet but I will when I go down and I'll let you have the purchase order number."

"Good, that's a nice job to check it out on. Do that, mate. O.K.?"

Ron processed the purchase order, worked out how long the job should take, checked on the last time it was done, for time, and to see if it was short of material. It wasn't and he then ordered the material from South Essex Steel, as before, and gave all the information to Jill to pass on to the boss. Jill was obviously aware of the problem and left the information on Bill's desk.

The following morning, on arriving at the office, Ron's first thought was to look and see if the Watkin's job had been scheduled. It had and the material was due in by the afternoon. After checking to see that no other jobs had been short during the night, he waited until just after nine o'clock to 'phone up to Jill to pass the information on to the boss. Much to Ron's surprise, she hadn't arrived, her 'phone just rang and rang. Ron replaced his handset thinking 'she'll be in later and I'll speak to her then.'

By mid-morning, Bill Ross had phoned down twice to ask if anyone had heard from Jill. No-one had. Brian, in his usual tactful manner on hands free, suggested that someone should contact Johnny Gibbs, only to have the 'phone put down on him, causing Mick and Ron to grin at each other. Brian was aware of the monitoring of jobs that was going on. Sitting opposite Ron, it was hard not to notice the extra care that was being paid to each job and he was trying to get in on the act and was helping as much as he could.

"Your material for Watkin's has arrived, Ron, do you want to go and check it off yourself," Porkie shouted round the door of the office. Ron thought at first that Porkie was being sarcastic but he wasn't, he genuinely was trying to help. Which is just the reaction that Bill Ross had hoped for when he called the meetings.

"No, but make sure the forklift driver is careful when he counts them, please," Ron replied. "Thanks."

Ron waited for the packing note for the Watkin's material and, checking that everything was correct, took it upstairs to Jill's office.

Jill's desk was still empty. Bill's office door was open. He looked in the doorway.

"Come in, Ron," said Bill. "I don't know what's happened to Jill today, she hasn't turned in and I've 'phoned her several times but I can't get an answer. Unlike her."

"Did you get the all the information about the Watkin's job that I left with Jill?"

"Yes, thanks. I've done a calculation on the material cost for that job and if they don't run short, the cost of material will be fourteen per cent and, with machine time, we should come in at about fifty two per cent gross, which is as it should be and that's allowing for a slight rise in the cost of the material."

Ron unfolded the paper work he had been fiddling with. "This is the packing note for the steel. It's just arrived and the delivery's been checked by Porkie and the fork lift driver."

"Right, put it on Jill's desk and when she gets here, I'll get her to list it. When's the job going to be cut?"

"It will be going on this evening and should be finished by midday tomorrow."

"Good, keep an eye on it, mate."

Ron returned to the ground floor, walking past Jill's empty desk. He placed the packing note from South Essex Steels under the paperweight which held all her outstanding jobs. He thought to himself 'I wonder what she's up to.'

Porkie was talking to someone on the phone when Ron walked back into the office, telling them how he alone had caught Robby fiddling thousands of pounds from Precision Laser and how he would have thumped him if he hadn't been restrained. He moderated his tone when he realised that Ron was listening to the conversation. Ron couldn't help smiling.

Johnny Gibbs' car pulled into the car park. Porkie saw it through the window. He waited until he saw Johnny get out then banged on the glass so hard that the frame shook. Johnny looked towards the vibrating window to see Porkie, with exaggerated gestures, beckoning him to come to the office by way of the dispatch department, instead of his normal way by the executive block. He acknowledged Porkie's signal with a little wave and, carrying a roll of drawings and his brief case, made his way to the dispatch entrance. Letting the office door slam behind him he walked in, looking straight at Porkie as much to say 'what's the panic', Porkie, with his usual loud voice and his normal lack of diplomacy, said, "What have you done with Jill? She ain't turned up for work and the boss has been trying to get hold of her."

Johnny's face was evil. He looked round the room to make sure that what he was about to say wasn't going to be heard by anyone of importance and in a slow, definite tone said, "Look here, you nosy bastard, I'm not her bloody keeper and even if I was, I certainly wouldn't tell you my plans. Jill's a person in her own right and has a life of her own and if it's any of your damn business, which it's not, I haven't got a clue where she is." He stuffed the roll of drawings further up under his armpit and, putting his brief case down momentarily to open the door to the other office block, slammed the door behind him and was gone.

Poor old Porkie still sat there with his mouth open. He hadn't meant to upset anybody and was only trying to be helpful but, as usual, he had said the wrong thing at the wrong time.

Bill Ross heard Johnny come in and in a very different manner said to him, "Jill's not turned in today and she hasn't 'phoned in either. I don't suppose you know what's happened to her?"

"No, they've just told me downstairs she's not in. I don't know where she is."

"Right." He then proceeded to ask Johnny how things were going, businesswise, and how many orders from Albion International were expected this month. They chatted for several minutes before Johnny went to his own office to start quoting for the large roll of drawings he had bought in with him.

The Watkin's job ran to time and, after closing down the job card and checking that the material had not been short, Ron took the completed paperwork through to the accounts department. Having let them process their side of the job, he then took the job card and the machine report to Jill for analysing.

Jill's desk was still empty, the packing note from South Essex Steel, that he placed there yesterday, was exactly where he left it.

"No, she's still not in," shouted Bill from his office. He could see Ron from his office door, which he had deliberately left open because of the absent Jill so that he could oversee her job as well as his own.

Ron walked into the open office. "Have you heard from her?"

"No, I'm getting worried. It's not at all like her to behave like this."

The two men sat and went through every aspect of the

Watkin's Engineering job. It didn't take long. Everything checked out perfectly. In fact there was almost an entire sheet of material over and the whole job worked out at the correct gross profit.

"Well we're not losing that way mate, are we?"

"No," replied Ron. "What now?"

"I don't know, we'll have to wait and see if the auditors dig anything up."

"Ron, I know you and Brenda have met Jill socially. I don't know what you think but do you think that Brenda might go round to Jill's on the off chance, to see if she can find out what the hell's going on. I've 'phoned her several times and got no answer but the first time I 'phoned someone did pick up the receiver but wouldn't talk. I know that as her employer I should go round there, but I don't want to. If the girl is in some sort of trouble, she might find it embarrassing to talk to me about it."

"Yes, she'll go, I'll take her. I won't get involved. I'll let Bren go in and I'll wait outside. Before we go, have you said anything to Johnny Gibbs? He should know more than anybody. He's been friends with her for some time?"

"No, I haven't. I got the distinct impression from Jill a couple of weeks ago that things between them weren't going too well."

"Right. I shan't be going to the Hare and Hounds tonight. I'll go straight home, have a bit of tea and then we'll go round there. Second Avenue, number eight, isn't it?"

"Yes that's right. Thanks once again, mate, please don't leave it too long before you go, I've a funny feeling that everything round at Second Avenue is not right."

"No, I know you are worried. We'll go straight after tea. As it happens I'm a bit worried myself."

Chapter 23

Jill was a young woman in her late twenties, blonde, slim and although not beautiful was, in a strange way very attractive. She had a certain something that was hard to explain. She wasn't tall, neither could she be called short. She had never been married but in her late teens had what she thought was a serious relationship with a young man from the college that she was attending. They spent the summer together and, after the relationship cooled a little, to her alarm she discovered that she was pregnant. Her parents were elderly and very old fashion, still living as they had been brought up, very prim and proper. They couldn't come to terms with the shame their only daughter had brought on their household. The young man, when he found out that Jill was pregnant, avoided the situation. He never stood by her but instead got involved with one of her college friends. She never forgave either of them. During her pregnancy her mother was taken seriously ill with cancer and after a fairly short time, died. Jill was taken into hospital in heavy labour, at the time of her mother's death. She lost the baby and resigned herself to staying at home and looking after her elderly father. Her father, being an ignorant and stubborn man, blamed Jill for the death of his wife and, at first, made Jill's young life hell, but she looked after his every need and gradually won back her father's love until he died about five years later. After the death of her father, she took a long time to come out of her shell. She was left the house at

Second Avenue and a small amount of money. There was no-one in her life and she started work at Precision Laser as a clerk in the accounts department. She put all the effort into her job that she had put into her father's care. She became a valuable part of the team at Precision Laser and was eventually promoted to the job of Bill Ross's secretary. She purchased a small car and started to take driving lessons and life began to open up for her. She was gradually brought out of her shyness and her quiet ways by the team at the firm and in a strange sort of way, Porkie, in his crude outlook on life, had contributed to her being able to take a laugh and a joke. He never pulled any punches in what he wanted to say, as crude or as rude as it was, and eventually she could give as good as she got.

Johnny Gibbs was working in the same area as Jill and, having a company car, played up to her. She, from her very sheltered background and knowing that Johnny was single, thought he was some sort of knight in shining armour but not being ready for romance, kept him at arm's length for a long time, until about the time when the factory moved to Lower Street. When, one late summer evening, Johnny had been helping move the paperwork files from the old premises to the new after hours, so as not to disturb the daily routine too much, Jill was also staying behind to lay out the offices and make ready for the next day. Johnny invited Jill for a drink on the way home, to lay the dust as he put it. She, not sure what to do, agreed to go with him and he, being much more worldly than her, took her to all his regular haunts, where he was, of course, well known. She wasn't used to being with someone so popular and being treated so well. They became friends and began to meet on a more regular basis.

The company had a small stand at Sub-contractors Exhibition at Earl's Court. The exhibition lasted five days and it was Johnny Gibbs' job to run and man the stand, with help from anyone who could be spared from the office. Johnny would oversee the stand and the helpers would hand out leaflets and, if any technical information was required, they could call on Johnny to take over and answer the more technical questions. Almost everyone in the office took their turn and Jill was included on the rota. When it came to Jill's turn to go, she was picked up at home by Johnny and driven to Earl's Court. The size of the exhibition overwhelmed her and at the end of the day, which was a very long and tiring day, Johnny turned on his usual charm and persuaded Jill to stay in London for a meal. After the meal and after two bottles of red wine, both in a very relaxed and happy mood, they walked through Kensington, like young lovers, hand in hand, Jill enjoying every minute of Johnny's company.

On the drive home Jill giggled and sang like a naughty schoolgirl. Johnny was nowhere near as intoxicated as Jill, but if he had been stopped by the police he would have failed the breathalyser test. That seemed to add to the excitement of the evening. During the journey, Johnny would, as a matter of course, touch Jill's thigh, through her dress, during his conversation. The first time he did it, she went quiet but he just carried on chatting away as though nothing had happened. Then, as before, he would give her knee a little squeeze and after a couple of times she took no notice at all.

When they arrived at Jill's house, Johnny drove straight in to Jill's driveway and said that he had time for one quick coffee and then must go. Jill didn't even know how to say 'no' and was quite happy to invite him in. As she put the key into the door she felt Johnny's hands on her waist as if to support her and as the door opened he followed immediately behind, grabbed her, twisted her round and, kicking the door shut with his foot and before she could put the lights on, kissed her passionately on the lips. That moment they both knew it was inevitable.

A few weeks passed and the lovebirds lived in each other's pockets. They spent all their spare time together. Johnny had said that it was better that the people at work didn't know, at least for the time being, but Jill wanted to tell the world. They didn't go out much and stayed together most of the time at Jill's house in Second Avenue. Johnny thought it best not to use his house in Orchard Avenue in case old Ron and Brenda next door should happen to notice. When they did go out, it was right out of the area and Johnny would let her drive some of the time to try and get her ready for her driving test, but only in her car or the firm's company car, never in his prized sports car. Jill loved his new sports car and they would occasionally go to the Romford Tennis Club. Johnny had a few friends at the club, one in particular who had the same car as Johnny's and the same colour. His name was Bartholomew Tornton, Bart for short. He was a man of about the same age as Jill, very well mannered and very well spoken. He was the son of Jonathan Tornton, who had retired and left the small steel business to his son to manage. Bart gave the outward appearance of being extremely wealthy, he always had very beautiful girls with him and he spent a lot of time away, horse racing. Jill never saw Johnny or Bart ever play tennis, they just used the club to meet each other. He and Johnny were always talking out of earshot of Jill and they obviously had a business interest together. There was no shortage of money with Bart and on several occasions Jill noticed Bart giving Johnny several twenty pound notes. During one of the early trips to the tennis club, Bart produced a packing note from Jonathan Tornton Steels Ltd, to Precision Laser Ltd., showing that thirty sheets of steel had been delivered.

He handed the note to Johnny and said "my stupid driver forgot to get this signed this morning and to save any embarrassment, put your signature there and I will take our copy to the office tomorrow." Johnny made a squiggle on the paper and handed the packing note to Jill.

"Here you are, sweetheart, put that in your bag and you can process it tomorrow." Jill thought it odd but did as she was told. On the way home, Jill sat with her head back on the headrest, with her eyes closed, listening to the radio. As the night air was cold, Johnny had put the soft top up and he slowed right down and said, "I've been thinking, wouldn't it save a lot of money if you sold your house and moved in with me? We would be financially secure and we could halve our expenses."

Jill, turning the radio down, looked at him, smiled and said "I've had exactly the same thought. Do you mean get married?"

"Well, eventually, of course," he smiled and gave her knee a little squeeze.

Jill was over the moon and nothing mattered in the world. She'd got her Johnny and he was at last going to let the world see that they were a couple. The first couple to know were Ron and Brenda. Johnny had invited them in one evening for a drink, as they only lived next door. They had a pleasant evening but Brenda did make several remarks about Susan, Johnny's first wife. It was tactless of Brenda to mention Susan but Jill was so happy that nothing could upset her. Jill knew Ron from work. He had just started at Precision Laser and apart from Brenda making out she knew more about Johnny's house than her, she enjoyed the company.

The packing note situation with Bart happened two or three more times. Jill was completely unaware of what she was doing and innocently carried on authorising payments to Tornton's according to the paperwork, until the big investigation at work into the amount of money that was being spent on steel. Then she realised that what she was doing could have something to do with the company being overcharged for steel that, in fact, it was not receiving. She got very worried and approached Johnny about it.

Jill waited until the others in the office were either out or preoccupied before she went to see Johnny in his office. She tapped gently on the door.

"Come," was the answer. She opened the door. "Hello, love, what can I do for you?"

"Johnny, what's going on."

"What about?"

"I've been authorising payments to Tornton's on your say so. You told me that you had checked all the packing notes from downstairs, and the packing notes that Bart's been giving you I've had invoices for. I suspected they have been wrong, but because you said it was all right, I cleared them and paid them."

"What do you mean?"

"Come on Johnny, I'm not stupid, you have some sort of fiddle going with Bart Tornton. You two are up to something."

"I don't know what you mean. Have you said this to anybody else?"

"No, not yet. I've come to see you first, before I go and see Mr Ross."

"That would be a very silly thing to do."

"Why?"

"Why? I'll tell you why. You're the one who checks all the packing notes. You're the one who checks all the invoices. You're the one who is supposed to check that the material is for certain jobs and you're the one who authorises payment, so I reckon you are at the middle of any fiddle and you can't prove otherwise."

The poor girl just stood and looked at her lover. Never before in her life had she felt so much contempt for anyone as she did at that moment for Johnny Gibbs. The colour drained from her face, her eyes glazed over. With a little tear running down her cheek, she turned and left the room.

Although Johnny was extremely embarrassed at being found out, he, in no uncertain terms, made it known to Jill that she was involved and that no-one would believe her if she didn't keep quiet. Jill finally realised that she had been used. She had thought of going to the boss about what she knew but realised that she, through her ignorance, was as guilty as anybody. She knew that any relationship with Johnny was over. She felt numb, she felt anger, she felt hatred. She didn't know what to do. After giving the problem a lot of thought, her decision was to get away from the atmosphere of the office, get away from Johnny Gibbs, be on her own and think it through.

She moved all her belongings out of Johnny Gibbs' house and moved back to her own home at Second Avenue. She was devastated, her faith in human nature had once again been destroyed. Her telephone was unplugged and she cut herself off from the outside world until she could get her brain back into gear.

Chapter 24

Ron briefed Brenda on what was going on at the office and that Bill Ross had asked if she would make a call at Jill's house. She didn't mind a bit, she quite liked Jill. They decided to take Ben for a walk up Second Avenue and, as they passed the house in which Jill lived, they would give her a knock and Ron could carry on walking Ben while Brenda would go in and try to find out what the matter was.

It was still dark in the evenings at that time of year and old Ben must have thought it was his birthday to be taken out by both his master and his mistress at that time. As they approached the house where Jill lived, they could see no signs of life, no lights on and the whole place in darkness. Ron stood with Ben at the driveway entrance while Brenda went up to the door and rang the bell. She could hear the door chimes ringing inside the house and the figure eight of the door number shone in light of the street lamp. No answer. She rang again and waited. Still no answer. She looked back at Ron, who, by now, was thinking it was a waste of time. He beckoned her and said, "You come and hold Ben and I'll go and have a look round the back."

He gave the lead to Brenda, which made Ben wag his tail and walked down the side of the house to the side gate, closely watched by Ben. The latch was rusty but the gate opened easily. Going round to the back of the house it was very dark. Ron looked in the patio window. Total darkness, only the light of the street lamp could be seen, shining through the front door glass panel showing that all the inside doors were open. Everything seemed all right except for the lack of Jill. The light in the kitchen of the house next door was shining onto the side of Jill's house. Ron thought he would give them a knock to see if they knew where Jill had gone.

He went back to the front of the house, after shutting the gate, told Brenda his plan and knocked on the door-knocker of the house next door.

"Hello, I'm sorry to disturb you, but I'm a friend of Jill's from number eight and I was wondering if you know how I can contact her."

The old man, who had answered the door in his dressing gown, said, "No. She was there a couple of days ago, but we have not seen her since. She is probably at Mr Gibbs' or she may have gone to see her Aunt who lives in Tilbury."

"Oh, right, thanks, sorry to disturb you. Bye."

Ron had no idea how to contact the aunt who lived at Tilbury and gave up. He knew that she wasn't at Johnny Gibbs'. They returned home and Ron phoned Bill Ross to tell him that he had discovered nothing. Bill's reply was that if she didn't turn up for work tomorrow, he would have a word with the local police, to see if they could throw any light on her disappearance, as now, he was beginning to worry as to what could have happened to her.

Next morning and no sign of Jill. After talking to Johnny Gibbs and being unable to get from him any information, Bill phoned the local police station. As Bill wasn't a relation, they seemed to treat the unusual behaviour as something quite matter of fact but promised to make some enquiries and phone back. Several people in the firm were expressing their concern about the disappearance of Jill, not least of all Johnny Gibbs, who, from his manner of late, was obviously under some form of pressure and came over as a bit touchy. Jill's behaviour was beginning to worry him.

"Ron, can you spare me a minute?" It was Bill Ross 'phoning down, his voice a bit sharp, and Ron could sense something was amiss.

Ron shot straight upstairs and into the open door of Bill's office. "Sit down, Ron, shut the door."

Ron had thought that he had been summoned for some information about Jill but Bill's face was tense and in front of him was the invoice ledger for invoices paid.

"Ron, why do you nearly always go to Torntons for your steel, when we get a bigger discount from South Essex, or Armitage's, or even Brown Brothers?"

Ron looked blank. "I didn't know I did, I usually phone round for the best price and delivery. I do give some orders to Tornton's, but not many."

"Well, would it surprise you to find that nearly forty eight per cent in December, and fifty four per cent in January of all the steel we used came from Torntons?"

"Yes, it would. I don't use them that much."

"Ron, we've paid them over sixty thousand pounds over the last nine weeks and that's a lot of money by anybody's standard."

"Well, I haven't ordered that much. It must be Porkie and we never use them for stock orders. The only time I ever use them is for a last minute rush order, if I can't get it quicker from someone else." Ron sat and thought. "I'll prove it, let me go and get my purchase order book. I'll show you how many times I've used them."

"O.K., fetch all the order books up, including Porkie's, and Mick's, if he orders any material."

Ron disappeared to get the paperwork that was going to prove Bill wrong. Having collected all the order books, walking up the stairs on his way back to Bill's office, he flicked through the pages of Porkie's order book, hoping to find orders made out to Tornton's Steel but in the very quick flick through, he couldn't see any. On returning to the office, he found the door closed. He heard voices coming from inside the closed door and waited for a few minutes. Eventually he knocked on the door and waited.

"Yes, who is it?" came Bill's voice.

Ron opened the door and, to his surprise, sitting in the

chair that a few minutes before he had vacated, was Detective Sergeant Frost.

"Come in, Ron, you had better listen to this," said Bill.

Ron pulled another chair up, after putting down the books from downstairs on the end of Bill's desk. He smiled at the Police Sergeant, noticing he had the same tie on as the last time they met. Both Bill and the policeman were very subdued. They waited until Ron was ready, then the Detective continued.

"We have been round to number eight, Second Avenue and, although no answer was obtained at the door, after making enquiries at the neighbours, we forced open the garage and I'm sorry to say that inside we found the body of Miss Jillian Mary Spence. As far as we can make out, she had committed suicide. She was sitting in her car with a hose pipe connected to the exhaust." He waited for a second or two to allow what he had said to sink in, then carried on.

"There was an empty Paracetamol bottle and a half full bottle of vodka lying on the seat next to her. She must have been there for some time. The car engine had stopped because it had run out of petrol. The body has been identified by Mr and Mrs George Spence, the young lady's relatives from Tilbury. In the absence of a suicide note we are treating it as suspicious and a full investigation will now follow."

The room went quiet, you could have heard a pin drop. Bill was the first to speak, he cleared his throat and in an emotional voice said, "Thanks for coming to let us know. Is there anything we can do? What a waste of a young life. I don't know what to say."

"No, sir, nothing you can do, I'm afraid. Yes, it is a tragedy. I thought I had better pop in to tell you face to face. If you will excuse me, I do have to go back to Second Avenue to carry on trying to find out why a young girl like that would take her own life, which I think she did."

"Of course." Bill rose with the Sergeant, shook his hand, then in turn the policeman shook Ron's hand.

As he went to go, the policeman looked back and said,

"Do either of you gentlemen have any idea why a young lady like that would do a thing like this?"

Ron and Bill glanced at each other, as if to see who was going to speak first. Ron started. "No, all I can say is that she hasn't been herself of late, she's been moody and had certainly lost her usual sparkle." Bill agreed. The Sergeant thanked both men and promised to keep them informed should any further information come to light. He looked as though he was deep in thought as he left. He pulled the office door closed behind him and was gone.

They looked at each other, neither knowing what to say. Bill shook his head. "I don't believe it. What on earth would make her do that?" Ron grunted in sympathy with what Bill had just said. The purchase order books that Ron had run downstairs to get were still lying on the edge of Bill's desk. They didn't seem important any more. Ron began to flick through them, not reading them, his mind being on what he had just learned.

"Leave them Ron, I'll go through them when I get a minute. Will you excuse? I want to have a word with Johnny Gibbs." Ron got up and left as Bill was ringing Johnny's extension. He could hear him asking Johnny to come to his office as he closed the door behind him. At first, Ron dawdled on the landing, hoping to bump into Johnny Gibbs but then changed his mind and quickly went downstairs to the production office.

Chapter 25

When Ron walked back into the production office, it was empty. He sat down and tried to collect his thoughts. The first thing he did was to phone Brenda and tell her the terrible news and, while he was explaining to her what had happened, both Mick and Porkie returned. They couldn't help but overhear what was being said, and waited patiently for Ron to finish his conversation to his wife so that they could be put in the picture. In no time at all the news had spread all round the factory and little groups would accumulate by various machines, obviously talking about the sad event. It seemed to make work unimportant but jobs were still getting done, although not with the same enthusiasm.

"Where's that bastard off to?" said Porkie as he looked out the window. "I bet he's got something to do with Jill's death." Johnny Gibbs was getting into his car. He sat inside for a moment then started the engine. He was some way from the production office window but even from that distance you could see his face was very white and he was obviously upset. He drove out of the car park very slowly and disappeared towards town.

Porkie had always been a bit wary of Johnny. He had always seemed superior to Porkie, although, in truth, he was not. Their jobs were of equal status but Johnny had given Porkie a few hard times about delivery dates and quality, and their paths had crossed on many an occasion. Porkie had always ended up the loser, mainly because he had no decent command of the Queen's English and, when cornered, resorted to swearing and shouting and, of course, lying.

That evening, Brenda didn't want to stay in. She couldn't bear the thought of what had happened. They agreed to go to Ron's club but decided to walk and, just to be nosy, they went by way of Second Avenue so they could have a look at the house where Jill had lived. The house was still in darkness but a police blue and white perimeter tape was around the entrances that led to the building and a uniformed police constable was on duty outside the house. They walked by and increased their pace as the constable on duty looked at them.

"They are taking it very seriously," Ron said as they went out of earshot of the uniformed policeman who stood on the doorstep of number eight.

"Yes, and quite rightly so," Brenda came back with. "It's terrible and they have got to find out who killed her."

"It was suicide, Bren, not murder."

"We'll see," was the answer.

*   *   *   *

"Come up when you've got a minute, please, Ron," was the message that came over the phone's hands-free system on Ron's desk.

"Right."

"Come in and sit down." Bill's face was very serious but the tone in his voice was soft and patronising. The three or four purchase order books, that Ron had left the previous day, were in a pile, neatly placed at one end of Bill's desk. The ledger of invoices paid was open on the desk in front of him and Ron could see that about ten of the entries had been highlighted in pink with a special marker pen.

Ron sat and Bill started. "Firstly, Ron, I feel I owe you an apology. I was a bit short with you yesterday about Tornton's Steel. What I've discovered has shown me that you chaps are doing a good job down there. We've been taken for a ride and before the police get here I wanted you to know that there is going to be a lot of trouble and some heads are going to roll, not only in this company but at Tornton's as well."

Ron looked puzzled and moved on his chair uncomfortably as Bill went on.

"The purchase orders you have raised don't, in any way, correspond to the invoices that have been sent by Tornton's. The packing notes match the invoices, but no way have we had that amount of steel in from that company. The auditors have been called in to verify what I've discovered and I've called the police. You see, Ron, Jill has been responsible for checking the invoices and authorising payment and I believe this may have something to do with her death."

Both men were very quiet. Ron realised what Bill had said, although he didn't really understand. His brain wouldn't grasp the situation. Bill went on to explain that someone had been fiddling the paperwork to make it look as though the company had been receiving steel that didn't exist.

"And that can only be one of three people and the only one who has had the opportunity to force Jill to do something like this, at this office, is Johnny Bloody Gibbs."

Ron sat back in his chair. He couldn't look at Bill. He looked at the ledger that was open on Bill's desk in front of him and said "What do you mean? Johnny Gibbs killed Jill?"

"No, I mean Johnny Gibbs put her into such a position that she couldn't stop herself from helping him cheat us out of quite a few thousand pounds and that's why she took her own life."

"Brenda has never liked that shitbag and I know what she means now," was Ron's reply.

"When I called him in yesterday, to tell him what had happened, he appeared very upset so I sent him home. I've tried several times today to reach him by 'phone and I can't get an answer. I've told Detective Sergeant Frost my suspicions and he agrees with me that there is something for him to answer to. Also, he is going to visit Tornton's to see why we've been invoiced for steel that in no way we have received." Ron was finally coming to terms with the situation and the more he thought about it the more he got worked up inside.

Detective Sergeant Frost called to collect copies of all the paperwork appertaining to the transactions between the two companies. He insisted that all the originals must be made available for evidence. He was accompanied by a slightly younger man who was introduced as Sergeant Harrison, a member of the Fraud Investigation department. When all the paperwork had been examined by the two policemen, it became clear what had been taking place. In fact the fraud investigator said that the fiddle was so obvious that it should have been noticed much sooner.

Bill Ross agreed and said, "I've known Johnny Gibbs, and Jill, for years. I trusted them both implicitly. I treated them as friends. I can't believe they could pull a stroke like this."

The officer, in his wisdom, said, "Wherever there are goods and money transactions, you can't trust anybody all of the time." To which a mumbled acknowledgement was returned by Bill.

"Don't worry about Johnny Gibbs, we'll pick him up and then we'll find who is involved at Tornton's, although, if you have always paid your accounts by cheque then it's got to be someone who has access to drawing money from their company account," said Sergeant Frost. He then went on to collect all the paperwork and copies of bank statements that were available at that moment in time. They left in a funny sort of jovial mood. It was obvious that they knew they had got a cast iron case and they were getting excited about the thought of an arrest, from which, on the surface, it seemed that there was no way out.

A couple of days passed. Brenda was beginning to get on Ron's nerves. She seemed to spend all her time at the window, looking at the entrance to Johnny Gibbs' house next door. She was doing what she thought was right, to keep an eye on his place just in case he came home to collect something. Ron, with the help of Mick, had retrieved the company car, using the spare keys and taken it back to the firm. Johnny's new car, of course, was nowhere to be seen but the police had circulated the description of the car and the registration and of course the description of Johnny himself. Brenda kept her vigil on the house next door and she had actually gone into the house with the police when they turned up to inspect the premises, in the course of looking for Johnny. The whole area was buzzing with the news of firstly Jill's death and then of the disappearance of Johnny and Brenda became very popular as the main source of news on her more frequent shopping trips and Ben was getting many more daytime walks, to help Brenda spread the news. Ron, on the other hand, found the whole thing a bit distasteful and, for the time being, stopped his nightly call at the Hare and Hounds and even his club mates wanted him to exaggerate on what had happened to make it more interesting. So, for the time being, he was giving his weekly visit to the snooker club a miss as well.

Chapter 26

"Mr Ross, there's a gentleman to see you. He hasn't got an appointment but says it's very important that he speaks to you," said the receptionist over the intercom part of the telephone.

"Who is it?"

"A Mr Jonathan Tornton."

"Oh, right, you had better send him in." Bill quickly tidied his desk and, with a little apprehension, waited for the door to open.

"Good morning, Mr Ross, thank you for seeing me at such short notice. I know you must be a busy man." And with that, in walked an elderly man, immaculately dressed in a dark, pin-striped suit, with beautiful, silver, well-groomed hair and sporting a small, neat, silver-grey moustache. He carried a black walking stick with a gold knob and in his other hand he carried his hat, a navy blue trilby, and on the small finger of that hand was a large, diamond, solitaire ring.

He closed the door behind him and as he walked towards Bill's desk he said, in perfect English, with an accent that must have come from Eton or Harrow, "I felt that I must come to see you. Unethical it might be, but as my son has caused you so much distress, I thought the least I could do was to come and see you personally and try and offer you some sort of an apology."

The two men shook hands and Mr Tornton sat on the chair

in front of Bill's desk. He leaned his stick against the arm of his chair and, with his hat on his lap, sat back and started. "I don't know where to begin to tell you that what has happened has upset my wife and myself so much. We feel so ashamed. We have given Bart everything he wants and to do what he has done to you is unforgivable, to say the least."

"Thank you for that. I haven't really come to terms with the whole thing yet," Bill answered. Then he sat back to listen to what the elderly man had got say. He had no idea what was on the old man's mind.

"Yes, I can imagine," the old man answered, patronisingly. "You see, I have worked all my life to keep Tornton's Steel going and when Bart started with the firm, after he had completed his education, I gradually took a back seat and let him run the firm. Things haven't been easy and over the last three years, things have really slowed down and like a good many other firms, we have experienced a considerable cash flow problem. But that doesn't excuse the terrible thing that these two men have cooked up, to steal money from your company."

"No, you're right and, do you know, that as a result of what has happened, a young lady who has been working for me here, has taken her own life?"

The old gentleman looked down as if in disgrace and answered, "Yes, I do know and that's part of the reason why I came to see you. Both my wife and I are very upset over it. I know my son has to be punished and his credibility will suffer for many years to come. I'm not a wealthy man but I am an honest one. What my son has done, I will not tolerate. I intend to make good every penny that he has swindled you out of and have instructed my solicitor to contact your company and make arrangements for a settlement to be worked out. The money will come from the sale of assets which are owned by my son and if there isn't enough there, the balance will come from what he would have got as an inheritance from my wife and myself. As for the young lady, who so unfortunately found the only way out was to take her own life, I am indeed truly sorry and if there was something that I could do to reverse what has happened I would gladly do it."

Bill was taken by surprise at what the old man had said and, although he was still very uptight inside, what the old man had promised would certainly take the pressure off trying to come to terms with the loss of so much revenue. He tried to make the old man feel at ease by offering him a coffee. He refused and said, "When it is all over and things get back to normal, I would very much like to keep you as a customer and maybe, you will invite me back and show me round your plant." Bill agreed and the old man left, leaving Bill with the thought that perhaps everything was not as bad as it had first appeared.

Detective Sergeant Frost came to Bill's office to let him know that all investigations regarding the death of Jill were complete and that it was, in fact, suicide and that the body had been released so that the funeral could go ahead. The funeral arrangements were going to be made by Mr George Spence, the girl's uncle, who lived at Tilbury. Bill promised to 'phone him to see if he could help in any way.

Sergeant Frost was a bit annoyed that the father of Bart Tornton had been to see Bill. He said that the promises of reimbursement would only make the sentence lighter and that it was only done so that the fact would come out in court. Bill showed him the correspondence from the solicitors of Jonathan Tornton Steels Ltd., showing that reimbursement was being organised. He said that if they did get anything back, they would be very lucky. Bill wasn't so sceptical, he had more faith in the old man.

Chapter 27

Johnny was down in the dumps, he couldn't get his mind focused on his job. What he had done to that young girl was playing on his mind. Although he was a bit of a bastard, he didn't like the thought of deceiving Jill. He went to see Bart, who didn't really want to know. He was only interested in getting more money out of Johnny's company. Johnny ended up getting a bit tight at the tennis club after sitting and trying to drown his sorrows and, when closing time came, he was at a complete loose end.

Like a magnet, he ended up on Sue's doorstep. She was in bed, sound asleep. He rang the doorbell several times before she came to the door.

"What the hell do you want at this time of the morning?" She was dressed in a silky type dressing gown over her skimpy silk night-dress, and dainty pink matching slippers.

"I'm in a spot of bother. Can I come in? I've something to tell you."

"Do you know it's gone midnight?"

"Yes, but, please let me in. I won't be any trouble, I promise. You haven't got anybody in there with you, have you?" he said looking over her shoulder.

"No, course not, you can come in just for a minute, no trouble mind and only coffee."

Johnny followed her into the living room, his eyes looking round for signs of any male visitors. There weren't any. He sat on the settee and loosened the laces in his shoes while

Sue made a couple of mugs of coffee. She brought the mugs in and put one down beside Johnny. The other, she kept in her hand and sat down on one of the armchairs, with her hands cupped around the hot mug to keep warm.

"Well, what's so important that you've got me out of bed at this time of night, then?"

"I'm lonely and I've been stupid. I've got someone into a lot of trouble and I think she might do something silly."

"She! So you found yourself a girlfriend then?"

"She's not a girlfriend, as such, but we have been out together a few times."

"I suppose you've made her pregnant, you bastard?"

"No. Why do you women always jump to that conclusion? I haven't and even if I had, it wouldn't be any of your damn business."

"What are you doing at my house at this time of night then, when there's a bloody court order banning you from here? Why don't you piss off, you bastard and leave me alone."

With that Johnny jumped up and in his half-intoxicated state, slapped Sue across the face as hard as he could. She was taken aback by the speed with which Johnny had jumped up. Not knowing what to do and knowing she had the law on her side, she threw the remains of her coffee over him. It was still very hot and he, not being in complete control, grabbed her round the throat. He squeezed and squeezed until her eyes bulged, her face became extremely red. He couldn't stop himself. All the frustration of the last few years came rushing back. He had called to see her to try and sort out in his mind what he was going to do and ask for advice but all he was getting was abuse. 'The bitch', he thought, 'I've kept my side of the bargain, I've paid you all that money'. His grip was getting tighter and she was trying to break it. She kicked him and scratched his face. She was getting weaker and eventually she stopped struggling and moved no more. He let her limp body fall slowly on the floor. Realising what he had done, he tried to revive her but it was too late. He sat and looked at her twisted frame, half-naked, lying on the floor in front of him.

He knew that there was no way of covering this mess up. He panicked and ran out of the flat with his handkerchief in his hand after wiping his scratched face. He had no idea where he was going and quickly drove out of the area. He knew that now he was in real trouble and that it would only be a matter of time before the police would catch him. If only he had not gone to see Sue tonight, if only he hadn't been drinking, if only he had never met Bart Tornton, things could have been so different.

Chapter 28

Brenda was brushing Ron's jacket down, trying to remove the dog hairs that showed up against the black suit which he hadn't worn for ages, and Ron was making sure that what Brenda had on was appropriate for a funeral. Not that he had any worry on that score. Ron had been to work and come home again to change for Jill's funeral. A good many from Precision Laser were going to attend the ceremony. Not Porkie nor Mick, as someone had to stop and man the office and not many from the shop floor could attend. The ceremony was at St Mary's at two o'clock. Only the Spences were going to leave from the house with the coffin. The rest were going straight to the church.

As Ron and Brenda went into the church, the organ was playing very softly and slowly. That smell that only comes from churches was very prominent and as they walked in, Brenda's heels made a noise on the red-tiled floor of the aisle. They recognised most of the people in the church, nearly all from Precision Laser. Bill and Marion stood at the front with two very elderly-looking people, who must have been the Spences. The service was very moving and emotional but was over quite quickly. The vicar made a very short speech about the sad life of Jill and reference to the death of her parents when she was still a very young woman. Bill Ross, in a very touching tone of voice, read a short passage from the Bible. As the coffin, a light, teak colour with big ornamental brass handles and just one simple spray of pink and white carnations on top, was taken out to the graveyard, followed by the few mourners, they passed the couple who sat at the back of the church, who both just gazed at the altar. They were Mr and Mrs Jonathan Tornton, who didn't say a word to anyone. He had a tear in his eye and she had a handkerchief clutched in her hand and held up to her face. After the service, they left, without going to the graveside, as if they felt they were intruding on a very private ceremony.

In the church yard, not too near to the party that stood round the grave while the vicar completed the funeral, stood Detective Inspector Frost. He made himself as inconspicuous as possible and when the ceremony was all over and people were leaving, he waited until Bill and Marion had given their condolences to the Spences before attempting to talk to them. By this time, Brenda and Marion, and Ron and Bill were all engaged in conversation. As they walked in a group of four out of the churchyard, he approached the group.

"Good afternoon, folks," was his opening gambit. "Not a very nice occasion but I've got news that I think will please you all." They continued as a group until they reached their cars with the policeman walking behind them. When they reached their cars they stopped. Then the policeman continued.

"Mr John Gibbs has been arrested by the Metropolitan Police, at Islington in North London. He has been charged with the murder of his wife, Mrs Susan Gibbs, whose body was discovered at an address in Finchley three days ago. He has confessed to the crime and asked for the fraud at Precision Laser to be taken into account, to which he has also confessed. He also went on to say that Miss Jill Spence had no knowledge of what she was doing, or what she was getting herself into. I'm sure that on this occasion the powers that be will prosecute," he said, sarcastically, looking straight at Bill, knowing that the last time their paths crossed, a prosecution should have taken place.

Bill turned to Ron in front of the policeman and the two

women and said, "Ironic, isn't it, that although he can't be charged with the death of Jill, he is going to be done for murder anyway?"

Chapter 29

Over the next few days the atmosphere at Precision Laser was very quiet and subdued. Everyone, although they didn't all come into contact with Jill in their jobs, knew, or knew of her, but everybody had had contact with Johnny Gibbs and the rumours about his arrest and his crimes were the main topic of conversation between most of the shop floor staff and customers. It seemed that everyone wanted an account of what had happened.

Porkie was in his glory. He spent most of his time on the telephone, keeping all the regular customers up to date with the information of Johnny's arrest and of how he knew all the time that Johnny Gibbs was a crook and now that he had been charged with murder, how it only went to show what an excellent judge of character he was.

The police, Sergeant Frost and his accomplice, Harrison, made several calls to the factory to tie up the loose ends in the prosecution of Johnny Gibbs. As time went on it became more and more obvious that the fiddle perpetrated between Johnny Gibbs and Bart Tornton was going to have to take a back seat. The murder of Susan was going to be the main case that the police were going to have to deal with. The prosecution for the feeble fiddle which had cost Precision Laser so much money was to go ahead, but without the presence of Johnny Gibbs, although he was going to be tried but not for the moment. But the two police officers still had to gather all the evidence in order to prosecute Bart

Tornton. Bart Tornton had been relieved of his position at Jonathan Tornton Steels and his father had taken over the running of the company again and immediately the small steel stockholders' business began to increase. Jonathan Tornton was very well known in the steel distribution industry and it soon became very obvious to him that the way his son had been running the business left an awful lot to be desired.

Bill Ross had a lot of confidence in the elderly managing director at Jonathan Tornton's and, because of what had gone on between the two firms, made a special agreement with him that, providing the cost of the material was within two or three per cent of their competitors, Precision Laser would give them their custom, in return for a quantity discount at the end of each month.

The arrangement worked out for both companies very well and over the next few weeks Bill and the elderly Mr Tornton, became very well acquainted. Bill learned a lot from the old man about customer loyalty and customer satisfaction. The old man giving Bill an insight in to business that he had not appreciated before. The two of them became quite good friends.

Bill's company accountants had been in regular contact with the solicitors of Tornton's Steels and an agreement had been worked out for the reimbursement of the money that had been stolen from Precision Laser. It amounted to forty-six thousand pounds. When Bill received the letter offering this amount from Tornton's solicitors, he telephoned the old man.

"Mr Tornton, I've received the offer from your solicitors this morning and I thought I should 'phone you to thank you for the very gentlemanly way in which you have dealt with the problem."

"Yes, thank you for telephoning. It is my intention to raise a cheque for the amount stated and have it sent to you straight away. I'm sure you will have no objection to me having a copy of the offer sent to the solicitors who are concerned with the prosecution of my son, in the hope that it may do some good in his defence?"

The 'phone went very quiet. Bill thought for a moment. He thought of what Detective Frost had said about getting a shorter sentence if he was to accept any reimbursement and said "Mr Tornton, you have been very fair with me. What your son has done has taught me a big lesson in human nature. I know you are very upset and you must do what your heart tells you. I have no objections to you doing what you think you must do, to help your son."

"Thank you, you see I know what he done was very wrong but I've punished him. I've taken away his job, I've taken away his self esteem and, most of all, I've taken away any future he had in this industry. I'm not getting any younger and at my age I can see good in most people and I'm sure he is extremely sorry for his actions and I would like to think that, when I go, he will carry on the Tornton name in some capacity."

"Who knows, Mr Tornton, he may surprise you yet."

When Bill put the phone down he thought to himself 'I'm lucky to be getting my money back at all and the old man deserves a break but Bart must be punished for what he helped to do to Jill.' He also wondered if, in fact, Bart had really learned his lesson.

To fill the gap made by Jill's unfortunate death, Marion had stepped in to do her job temporarily. She took over all Jill's duties and many more. Ron found her very efficient and got on very well with her method of working but poor old Porkie found her hard work, she wouldn't let him get away with anything. Because she was the boss's wife he couldn't browbeat her like he used to the other girls in the office and he had to pull his socks up in his behaviour and his personal appearance.

Ron and Bill met that evening at the Hare and Hounds on the way home from work and Bill told Ron of the 'phone conversation he had had that day and how they were going to get reimbursed for that which had been stolen by Johnny Gibbs. Bill was very surprised to learn that Bart Tornton was, in fact, still working for Tornton Steels in the capacity of salesman and that Ron spoke to him on many an occasion to place orders with the company. Ron admitted that, at first, he didn't know who he was talking to but as time had gone by he had got to know Bart Tornton on the 'phone and the two of them had become quite good telephone friends. Bart Tornton was very wary of people's opinions of him, after what had happened and was keen to make amends. Ron told Bill. Bill's reaction was that he was entitled to feel very wary.

Ron made Bill laugh when he told him about the time that Porkie had said he was involved in the story to Tornton's Steels, about how he had solved the mystery of the missing metal and that he had given the police the vital information to arrest Johnny Gibbs and Bart Tornton and then discovered he was actually talking to Bart Tornton. The two men had a good laugh and it seemed just like old times.

Porkie at that moment walked in and, as was his normal behaviour, waited to be bought a drink. He would love to have had a moan about Marion but hadn't got the guts. Anyway, he had been warned previously about talking shop whilst Bill and Ron were playing pool. He contented himself by entertaining the others, who would listen to him in the bar, about his part in the capture of Johnny Gibbs. He had related the story so many times that he was beginning to believe it himself. He suffered no embarrassment that both Bill and Ron could hear him and that they knew the truth. They just smiled at each other and let him carry on in his world of make-believe. Gerry, the landlord at the Hare and Hounds, got to know Ron and Bill quite well from their regular visits to the pub. He knew the truth about what had happened at Precision Laser and he would also smile with the other two at Porkie's elaborate account of what had happened. They all knew that soon he would tire of telling the same story and would come out with something even more far fetched.

Ron and Bill's friendship strengthened as things at the office started to improve and the firm finally began to recover from the events of the last few months. Their social lives became more entangled and the nightly competition on the pool table continued, giving them something to rib each other about but they both would feel a lot better when the trial was over and all the police involvement was behind them. It seemed like a cloud was lingering over them while they waited for the court case to come up.

Chapter 30

Marion opened all the mail and recorded in a ledger every letter that arrived. Bill gave her a free hand in the office to reorganise the way things were done, to prevent anything of a similar nature happening in the future to that which had caused the upset with Jill. The cheque from Tornton's Steel arrived for forty-six thousand, two hundred pounds, much to Bill's delight. He looked at it for some time and turned to Marion and said "Do you know, love, that old man Tornton really is a gentleman? I was doubtful that we were ever going to receive this. He need not have paid it because it was down to his son and if it had been left to the courts we probably wouldn't have got any thing."

"Yes, I know but the fact we have been reimbursed must help when he eventually goes to court."

"So what, I think he has probably learned his lesson and we've got our money back."

Marion didn't answer. She was more interested in getting the cheque banked to see if it would clear. Bill knew it would.

Johnny Gibbs went to trial at the Crown Court at Chelmsford. It was a very much cut and dried case, although it became very emotional. He pleaded not guilty to murder, but guilty to a lesser charge. At the end of the trial he was sentenced to seven years detention in one of Her Majesty's Prisons. Bill, out of interest, attended the court a couple of times while the trial was on. It was a very different Johnny Gibbs he saw in the dock to the man he had known at Precision Laser. He had lost a lot of weight and his face was much thinner. Johnny had seen Bill in the court room but couldn't look at him. The Spences were also in court. He couldn't look at them either

The Spences, although getting on in years, had done quite nicely from the unfortunate death of Jill. As they were the only relatives, they had inherited Jill's house at Second Avenue and the rest of Jill's belongings. Bill stood and passed the time of day with them. They were very bitter about what had happened to Jill but the fact that they had been left the house in Jill's will had made their old age a little easier. They made it clear to Bill that they were very grateful for the inheritance but they could not possibly live in that house where she had been found and that they would continue to live in their council house at Tilbury. Bill understood and agreed with them, knowing that at their time of life any sort of change would be an awful upheaval for them. They made no comment about the sentence that was given to Johnny Gibbs. They told Bill that they had met him on two or three occasions with Jill, when the pair had called in while Jill was having some tuition in driving. They both said they had not liked him and that they knew he was no good. Bill only told them that he had always thought that Johnny would go far in the world, because he could work hard and had the right sort of attitude to succeed and that he was very disappointed in the way in which things had turned out. The Spences thanked Bill for helping with Jill's funeral arrangements and they made their excuses and left to catch their bus back to Tilbury. Johnny Gibbs' brother was also in the court. He didn't have any contact with Bill but Bill could see the strong family resemblance and how upset the young man was.

After the trial the police wasted no time in bringing the prosecution of Bart Tornton and Johnny Gibbs to court for the fraud at Precision Laser. This case was heard at Basildon Crown Court. Old man Tornton engaged a top barrister to defend his son and Johnny Gibbs was also in court, guarded by two members of the Prison Service. The case lasted one and a half days. It took that amount of time for the prosecution to explain in simple terms what had happened.

Both men pleaded guilty but Bart's barrister gave a long address to the judge explaining how his client had been persuaded to do what he had done by Johnny Gibbs. Bill was called to give evidence and was made to feel that it could have been his fault that it was so easy to steal from his company. At the end of the day, the outcome was that Johnny Gibbs was to serve six months in prison, the sentence to run concurrently with his existing sentence. Bartholomew Tornton, in view of the circumstances and the fact that the stolen money had been returned, was let off very lightly and had to report once a week, because he was awarded one hundred and twenty hours community service.

Both Mr and Mrs Tornton were in court when the sentence was delivered by the judge. They both looked over to where Bill was sitting with Marion. As Bill's eyes met the old man's, he could see that he was embarrassed by the light sentence. Bill nodded to him, as much as to say 'what you did has paid off', and the two looked away again, leaving the old man to struggle with his conscience. After the trial was over, Bill introduced Marion to the Torntons. Bart stood with his parents in the entrance hall of the court house. It was the first time that Bill had spoken to Bart. Bart was very sheepish and made several requests to be excused but his father made him stay and suffer the indignity of listening to the old man apologise for his son.

Bart knew that this episode was the last straw and that his father would never give him another chance. He finally realised that it was time to toe the line and put his back into getting his life into some form of order. He made a conscious decision, mentally, to do everything he could to help put things right with his family and get the family business back on an even keel. He had a few skeletons in the cupboard and was not sure whether to bring them out into the open or keep them hidden altogether.

Bart was in his very late twenties. He had been married but was living apart from his wife, waiting for a divorce to be finalised. He was very handsome and knew it. He had many girlfriends waiting around for him. He still had his new sports car, which made Bill wonder where the money had came from that had been repaid to Precision Laser. Bill found it hard work trying to talk to Bart, he was obviously uncomfortable being in Bill's company after what had happened. Bill also noticed that Bart had a very likeable side to him. He had an air of confidence and he smiled profusely with his eyes, which made Bill see how easily Johnny Gibbs had been influenced by him and, in other circumstances, Bill could have been influenced by his charm also.

In the run up to the trial, Bart's wife had received a telephone call from a lady saying that Bart was mucking around with several different women. The outcome of which was that Bart's wife invited the caller to Bart's house. After a long chat and a lot of frank conversation, Bart's wife found out that the visitor, whose name was Jean, was also having an affair with Bart and that things were not going too well for the pair of them, so the two scheming women decided to catch him out. When Bart arrived home that evening, his wife asked him if he knew Jean and was he having an affair with her? Bart, rather taken by surprise at such a question and feeling a bit embarrassed, answered "Don't be stupid." He wasn't very convincing. She asked again,

"Of course I don't know any Jean. I've never heard of any one called Jean let alone have an affair with them."

"Oh, really?"

With that, Bart's wife opened the cupboard in the kitchen in which Jean was standing. "Oh, so you don't know this Jean then?"

Out stepped Jean, looking daggers and ready to have an argument.

The look on Bart's face was a picture. He had nowhere to hide and nothing to say. He just left the house and never went back, knowing he hadn't got a leg to stand on. Divorce proceedings were started against him immediately by his wife.

Bill stood chatting with Mr and Mrs Tornton for some time outside the court-house. Old man Tornton poured his heart out to Bill about his disappointment in his son.

"Look, Mr Ross, this is not the place to say what is on my mind. You may remember that you promised to invite me to look over your plant at some future time. Would I be impertinent if I invited myself along one day next week to see you and have a little chat?"

"Of course not, you're welcome at any time."

"Good, you'll excuse us then and I will telephone you and make an appointment to see you one day next week."

The old couple left. Bill couldn't help wondering what the old man had on his mind.

Chapter 31

Marion told Bill that Mr Tornton had phoned, that he was going to be at the factory just after lunch and that she had confirmed the appointment was in order. She was as curious as Bill as to what the old man had on his mind. Bill made several guesses but was unable to come up with anything that made sense. He did, however, get all the figures of the amount of business they were now doing with Tornton's Steel ready in case that was the reason for the visit.

At one o'clock sharp the old man's Daimler pulled into the car park. He was on his own and, as usual, was immaculately dressed and carrying his gold-topped walking stick and still wearing his trilby. Bill could hear him being polite to the receptionist as he made his way up the stairs and heard him talking to Marion in his perfect English outside Bill's office. Marion showed him in.

"Good afternoon, my dear boy," he said as he entered.

"Come in, sit down, Mr Tornton. Nice to see you," Bill answered.

The old man sat on the chair in front of Bill.

"Drink, Mr Tornton? Tea or coffee?"

"No, thank you. Now, Bill, may I call you Bill? I feel I know you well enough."

"Of course you may." Bill felt like saying 'may I call you by your Christian name' but thought better of it. 'It would seem disrespectful to call him anything but Mr Tornton', Bill thought to himself.

"Well, Bill, the reason for my visit. I don't wish to see your factory, I know that you run your business very professionally and that's the reason I am here. You see, I am not getting any younger and I need someone to take over from me when I retire, yet again. I have given Bart every opportunity to take over from me and you know the outcome of the last time. Something similar happened once before, but not so serious. I need a caretaker to keep an eye on what's going on. The problem I have is this, Bart has been in charge and everyone who works for me knows that he is my son, so nobody will put up any resistance to his scatterbrain schemes. He is now working as a salesman and making a good job of what he is doing but until he proves himself I can't trust him. I want someone of your capability to oversee things for me and my wife if any thing were to happen to me."

He stopped to watch the reaction on Bill's face, to see if he could detect any sign from Bill that he was interested.

"Mr Tornton are you asking me to run your business?"

"Yes, but not you personally. Have you got someone in your organisation that you trust implicitly, that you could put in there as a figurehead, who could run the business in conjunction with me for now and eventually take orders from yourself, until Bart is capable, or at least has learned some common sense?"

"Wow! That's a tall order and that's some idea. What makes you think that we know anything about steel stockholding?"

"You don't have to. I have an excellent team who know the business but Bart can bully all of them. I know the answer is to get rid of my son but all my life I have worked the business up for him to take over from me one day and I still want him to when he eventually grows up."

" That's not something I can give you an answer to straight away. I'll have to think about it."

"Of course, I'm sure we can work out a financial package that will be advantageous to us both. I even thought along the lines of maybe amalgamating the two companies. Give it some thought and let me know what you think."

"Yes I will, but why me? Why this company?"

"Well, I'll tell you. You remind me of myself. I started just like you a good many years ago. I also put everything on the line to start my company. I know what a struggle you must have gone through. I've made a lot of acquaintances in the engineering trade since I started but not too many friends. You, I regard as a friend. Since this trouble with Bart and the Gibbs fellow, my telephone has not stopped. After I made a few initial enquiries about your company, all the firms I deal with who know of you, not once have I heard anyone run you down or say anything detrimental about you. All those people can't be wrong."

"That's very flattering but you're asking me to do something that, at the moment, I can't get my head round."

"That's understandable. I'll leave you to think about what I've said. I'll telephone you tomorrow."

The old man made his departure, saying goodbye to Marion as he left the first floor and again goodbye to the receptionist as he went out of the building on the ground floor.

Marion didn't understand what Bill was trying to tell her about what Mr Tornton had proposed. She couldn't grasp the situation any more than Bill could. Bill kept turning it over and over in his mind and no matter which way he looked at it, it didn't make sense.

After much thought and discussion with Marion, Bill made enquiries about the financial status of Tornton's. He found that old man Tornton had, in fact, purchased the freehold of the premises and yard at the steel stockholders' business address and with the amount of stock they carried, the company as a whole was worth quite a bit. He had no doubt about the man's sincerity but still couldn't understand why he had singled out Precision Laser to help him in his plight.

"Ron, can you pop up and see me?" said Bill over the telephone intercom system.

Ron ran up the stairs to Bill's office.

"Come in, mate. Sit down. Are you sitting comfortably?"

"Yes."

"Right, I'm going to ask you something that I know you can't give me an answer to until you've spoken Brenda."

"Yes." Ron sat waiting.

"How do you feel about going to run Tornton Steels as a manager?"

"What! What do you mean, leave Precision Laser?"

"No, I mean go and work there with Mr Tornton to learn the ropes and then work under my supervision as manager of the company?"

"I don't understand, are you buying Tornton's?"

"No, but Mr Tornton has made me a proposition. He feels he needs our help and the financial side could be very rewarding for you. I can't give you any details at the moment because they haven't been finalised. So go home and discuss it with Brenda and let me know what you think."

"Blimey Bill, are you sure that I'm up to that sort of job?"

"Ron, when you started here you knew nothing of this trade and after a few weeks you were running the production office. I know you can do it, so have a bit more faith in yourself. Anyway, you won't be thrown in at the deep end and I will always be here to advise you if you need it."

Ron felt very flattered at Bill's confidence in him. He wasn't so confident himself but thought, 'what an excellent opportunity', and gave Bill his answer.

"I'll confirm it with Brenda but I'm sure she agree. I'll give it a go."

Brenda felt the same as Ron to start with, although apprehensive. She agreed that if that was what Ron wanted then he should go ahead and give it a go. She felt very proud of her Ron, fancy him being in charge of a big steel stockists.

Chapter 32

Several weeks passed. Ron had his feet firmly under the table at Tornton's. Old man Tornton was every bit the gentleman that Bill had said he was. Bart was resentful at first but he soon realised it wasn't Ron's fault and became very helpful. In fact, the whole team was behind Ron. The staff, it seemed, were relieved that Ron was there and that he spoke their language. Ron had been put completely in the picture by Bill and Mr Tornton although Bart never, for one minute, thought that his father would take this type of action and not knowing for certain if it was permanent or not, was always on his best behaviour and became quite friendly with his successor. Ron got on very well with Bart and Bart admired the way that Ron was running the company.

Ron spent some time on the shop floor, learning the ropes about transportation and the different types of steel, bar, sheet and girder. He was thoroughly enjoying his new job and was determined to make a go of it. Although he was in charge, he knew deep down that he was only a puppet for old man Tornton and was part of a plan to punish Bart.

Whilst going through the customer base one afternoon, he noticed a company called Upminster Laser who were ordering small amounts of sheet metal on a regular basis. He thought he knew most laser cutters in that area, so decided to look their account up. To his surprise the directors of the company were listed as Anthony Morrison and Julian Tebbs, two of the sods who were involved in the scam at Precision Laser.

Ron 'phoned Bill at Precision Laser straight away. "Bill, did you know that Julian and that Tony Morrison must have been successful in obtaining a loan to start a laser cutting company, because they are buying sheet steel from us here at Tornton's?"

"Yes, mate, I was aware. Several customers have 'phoned me and told me they have approached them for business but if they get only one customer I shall be damned annoyed."

"Oh, you knew?"

"Yes, and I've heard tell that Robby is working there as well."

"But I thought you had phoned Cooper's Finance and put them in the picture?"

"I did but I guess they never took any notice of me and gave them the loan anyway."

"Well I'm damned. What are you going to do?"

"Nothing I can do mate, too late but they're not going to find it easy. They've started off with a bad name and if they make a mistake, someone will jump on them."

"Well, from the amount of steel they are buying from us they aren't doing too well."

"Good. I've been informed that Tony Morrison has got a lot to answer for, he's only shopped his previous employer to the tax man, something to do with PAYE and the company has had a tax inspection."

"Really? What a nice character."

"Yes, and something else. One of his previous work-mates had an affair and made his girlfriend pregnant. The shit-bag sent a congratulations card to the bloke's wife with all the details on it."

"He didn't? What a nice bloke. Still, those sort of people usually get their comeuppance sooner or later."

"Well, let's hope it's sooner, then."

From that moment Ron kept a close eye on the account of Upminster Laser and he reported back to Bill all the transactions that they placed with Tornton's Steel.

Chapter 33

Two or three days later, at the offices of Tornton's Steel. "Ron, there's someone to see you," said the receptionist. "Are you able to see him?"

"Yes, send him in." He wasn't used to giving interviews but was getting the hang of it and was developing quite an air of superiority.

"Good morning, a courtesy call really," said the man who had just entered Ron's office. "We've recently opened an account with you and I thought the personal touch would be nice as I was in the area. My name is Tony Morrison. I'm the Sales Director of Upminster Laser. We haven't been going long and I wondered if we could be of mutual help to one another?"

"Really? Nice of you to drop in," Ron answered, hardly believing his ears and excitedly waited for the man to continue.

The man sat before him, opening his briefcase. He was quite small in stature, smartly dressed, dark-haired with extremely large eyebrows that almost met in the middle above the nose. His complexion was almost white against his dark hair and dark brows.

He had a sort of squeaky voice and started "We are new in the area but certainly not new to laser cutting. We have the most up-to-date machines available and my partner has been in laser cutting almost since it started in this country. If I leave you some of our sales literature, would you be able to leave them in your reception area for your customers to pick up? In return, I would gladly pass your sales information round to my customers on my travels."

"Seems a good idea," Ron answered then went on to say "Do you know Precision Laser at Lower Street, Chadwell. Are they in the same field as yourself?"

"Yes, I've heard of them but they are very much low tech compared to us," he answered, somewhat surprised.

"I hear they had some trouble there with staff thieving?"

"Yes, I did hear something about that. I heard that they were very underhanded in their detection of the staff. Very naughty."

"Oh?"

"Yes, they bugged the telephone lines. Not cricket, eh?"

Ron sat and thought for a moment. "Tell me, Mr Morrison, how would you go about catching staff that were thieving hundreds of pounds from you? Would you not think that bugging the telephone was fair in those circumstances?"

"Well, yes, I suppose I would," he answered looking very sheepish and some colour actually came into his cheeks. "Well, anyway, if you pick us up any business as a result of our leaflets in your customer area, I will see that you are properly rewarded and if any customer wants to pay in cash we can come to some arrangement about the VAT."

"Oh, really? So you are not sticking to the rules then?"

"Well, yes we are but on some jobs we can lose the VAT."

Ron was beginning to get out of his depth and was thinking to himself 'maybe this is the information that Bill Ross could do with'.

Tony Morrison was also feeling a bit uncomfortable and after feebly trying to crack a couple of jokes, dumped about thirty or so leaflets on Ron's desk and left.

Ron 'phoned Bill Ross straightaway to tell him of the encounter with the infamous Tony Morrison. Bill listened with hidden excitement as Ron told of how he had made the man blush and what he had said about dodging VAT.

"Really, Ron, did he say that?"

"Yes, why?"

"Because if that's what they are up to, they won't last in business two minutes. Someone will shop them and it might even be me."

Chapter 34

At the monthly meeting between Ron, Bill Ross and Mr Tornton, to check if every thing was going to plan and how sales figures were going, several topics came up for discussion. Firstly, Ron's report on the behaviour of Bart was extremely reassuring, which pleased old Mr Tornton. Secondly, business was on the increase and some of the deals that Ron had instigated were proving very profitable and he was congratulated by both of the other men. Finally, the subject of Upminster Laser was raised. Old Mr Tornton knew nothing of the details of the scam which had happened at Precision Laser and was amazed that they had got away with it and that they had actually started their own company. The old man sat for some time in deep thought. What was going on in that brain, nobody knew. After a while, he spoke very slowly and deliberately.

"I think these guys should be taught a lesson," he said. "I wonder how they would feel if someone was to make them the target for a rip off?"

"What are you getting at?" enquired Bill.

"I don't know but give me some time and I will let you know what is on my mind."

Bill had a lot of faith in the old man. He knew that the old man was very alert and couldn't wait for what the old chap was obviously turning over in his mind to be made known.

"Give me a little time and I'll come back to you," he said, as he got up and left the room.

Bill and Ron sat and conversed. They were in regular

contact with one another but the nightly visits to the Hare and Hounds had ceased. They were arranging to meet for a game or two, when the old man returned. He had a slight smile on his face. He sat back down and started,

"What do you think of this idea? Why don't we give them some work, small quantities but expensive? Let them have the work with the promise of much bigger quantities to follow. Let them put themselves into debt to produce the parts and then let them down, or do you think I am being too vindictive?"

Bill looked at Ron. "A good idea but how can we make it work?" he said.

"Don't worry about the details. Do you think I am being too bloody-minded," the old man said.

"No, not a bit. They asked for it. 'Specially for the expense they cost me afterwards when they smashed the place up. That has always stuck in my throat."

"Right, no more to be said. Leave it with me and I'll work out the details. It might cost us a few pounds but at least we will get rid of some of the bad blood in the trade." The old man left the room with a smile on his face. "I'm going to enjoy this," he said as he went out.

"Blimey, I wouldn't like to cross him," said Ron as the old man left.

"No," answered Bill with a big smile.

A couple of days passed. Mr Tornton 'phoned Bill several times to find out how the quoting side of the subcontract business worked and how prices were arrived at. Bill explained in the greatest detail exactly how everything worked and did comment to Mr Tornton that the method used at Upminster Laser would undoubtedly be the same, as the programme for quoting was originally stolen from Precision Laser.

"Tell me, Bill, do you have any jobs on at the moment that are expensive in small quantities, that I could use as a carrot to dangle in front of these rogues?"

Bill thought. "Yes, we do a job for a company called Zenith Conveyers. They have a regular call-off of twenty parts a month. They are cut out of oversize sheets and we only get two parts from each sheet, making the material cost very high."

"How much per part?"

"Cutting and material, round about ninety pounds per unit."

"How about letting them cut this job for the next two months, as a subcontract? They won't know who they are cutting it for and you can still inspect the quality before you deliver them to your customer. Zenith's, I think you said?"

Bill agreed. Although he wasn't sure what the old man was up to, he had every confidence in his ability to teach these upstarts a lesson.

"Right, I'll start to put things in motion, then. First of all, Bill, can you let me have a copy of the drawing for these parts? Make sure there is no company name on them. Let me have a copy that I can fax to them for quoting, or I might even go personally just to have a look at their set-up."

"No problem. You can have it this afternoon."

The old man telephoned Bill again in the afternoon. "Bill, I'm going to use you as a company reference to open an account with Upminster Laser. The name of the company seeking an account will be British Conveyers of Maidstone in Kent. There isn't such a firm and I'm relying on their greed that they won't check this. I know that it seems strange but I'm banking on the fact that you have an excellent name in the business and that they won't have the guts to contact you for a reference."

"I see, but they are going to want more than one reference. I don't know of any other company where they have compromised themselves."

"I do, Tornton Steels. If they contact my firm for references, they will receive a glowing reference signed by my son, who now hasn't the authority to sign anything."

"A bit risky, isn't it?"

"For them, if they don't check properly, yes. We have got nothing to lose but we can gain an awful lot of self-satisfaction and a load of free parts that you will be able to sell on to Zenith Conveyers. Are you game?"

"Of course. I can hear from the tone of your voice that you are enjoying this."

"Yes, I am. I don't like my friends being ripped off and if I can help put matters right, then at my age, it will be worth it."

Chapter 35

Mr Tornton drove into the communal car park at the small industrial estate where Upminster Laser was situated. He walked straight into the building that housed one solitary profile cutter, with two men standing operating the brand new machine. He noticed several pallets of finished parts waiting to be dispatched and, bold as brass, bent down and started to read the delivery addresses, hoping he could remember them so that he could tell Bill in case they were any of his customers.

"Can I help you mate?" said a voice from behind. The old man stood and turned to see a young man in overalls, carrying a large spanner and he noticed that he had an earring in each ear and was covered in dirt from working on the cutting machine.

"Yes, I hope so. I was given this leaflet advertising your company by a chap at Tornton Steels."

The young man took the leaflet. "Yes, that's one of ours. What can we do for you?"

"Sorry, I didn't catch your name?"

"Oh, sorry. My name is Julian Tebbs. I'm in charge here."

"Good! Then you are just the man I'm looking for. If I waited, would you kindly give me a quote for cutting twenty of these?" The old man produced the drawing that he had got from Bill.

"Yes, of course. Let me see. They are very large parts, aren't they?"

"Too big for you to handle?"

"Oh no, but they will have to be cut from extra large sheets. If you give me ten minutes I'll work out a price for you."

"Great, then I'll wait, thank you."

Julian scampered away to a small office at the front of the building, to work out on the computer how much each part was going to cost. He left Mr Tornton standing near the pallets where he had all the time in the world to memorise the names of the firms that Upminster Laser was supplying. The old man took out his note-book and made several entries.

After about a quarter of an hour, Julian returned with the drawing and an official typed quote and handed both documents to Mr Tornton. "There we are, sir, delivery would be about four days."

Old man Tornton read the quote. "Ninety-one pounds and seventy pence," he read aloud. "That's very good. If I were to give you an order for two thousand, how will that affect the price?"

Julian looked at the old man and, trying not to show any reaction said "I'll have to re-quote it but I would say that it would fetch the price per part down by about twelve per cent."

"So, you are saying that each part would cost me about eighty pounds. That's very good and what about delivery?"

"Well, that's something I would have to look into. It would depend on the availability of the raw material and the cutting time would be quite extensive."

"Yes, of course. Anyway, can I give you a purchase order now for twenty and have them collected next week? I realise you don't know me from Adam, so when I collect I'll pay you cash and in the meantime, if you give me the appropriate application forms I will apply to your company for a credit account."

"Certainly, Sir. You didn't give me your name or who you represent?"

"No, I didn't, did I? I'm sorry, my name is George

Marshall and I am the Managing Director of British Conveyors. We are based at Maidstone, in Kent." The old man produced a purchase order showing all the details he had just related and including the VAT number. He had produced the forged paperwork that morning on a computer back at the office of Tornton Steels. Even the VAT number was fictitious. "If you have any problems, please don't hesitate to contact me. I'll give you my mobile number, because I spend very little time at the office. I'm usually out all day on the road."

Julian quickly found the application forms for applying for credit and gave the old man the quote he had printed off.

"Thank you. My transport will be here next Thursday to collect and the driver will bring with him cash for the job which, by your quote, will be eighteen hundred and thirty-four pounds plus VAT, so he should have with him when he arrives, two thousand, one hundred and fifty-four pounds and ninety- five pence. Yes? That's a very competitive price. We had some of these parts cut a few months ago by someone else and the price was a little more expensive than what you have quoted. That's fine. See you next week and I'll make sure that the cash is there when we pick up. Two thousand one hundred and fifty-four pounds, not forgetting the ninety-five pence."

"Yes, that's correct, Sir." The two shook hands and the old man left.

The old man reported to Bill by 'phone, on his arrival back at Tornton's office. Bill was pleased to get a description of the Upminster Laser set-up and was quite put out when the old man gave him the list of customers that had parts waiting to go out from the dispatch area at the unit. Nearly all the names he mentioned were previous customers of Precision Laser. 'So, they are hurting our business', he thought to himself. Mr Tornton filled in the credit application and gave Bill's firm and his own as references. He put down his own bank with the wrong address as bankers and returned the form.

Sure enough, two days later, a credit enquiry was received

by Tornton's Steel about the creditworthiness of British Conveyers of Maidstone and a gleaming reference was sent back by return. In the meantime, an order for ten sheets of oversize five mil. mild steel was received and delivered to Upminster Laser by Tornton's. Nothing, however, was received at Precision Laser regarding any creditworthiness for any company, let alone Upminster Laser. Old man Tornton 'phoned Bill, two or three times every day to see if any thing had arrived regarding creditworthiness and after a week said to Bill "Well, son. I think they have fallen for it and now it's time for you to take your revenge."

A driver was sent with the cash in an envelope to pick up the twenty parts that had been ordered. The driver was Bart Tornton. He went in a plain van. All four laughed when Bart told the story of how the money was carefully counted as he loaded the van at the Upminster end.

Bill, Ron and Mr Tornton all paid attention as Bart told of the conversation between Julian and Tony Morrison as they counted the money.

"There, I told you so," said Julian, "and they are talking of ordering two thousand. That's worth over one hundred and sixty thousand."

"Yes, we'll see. I don't suppose we'll hear from them again," replied Tony Morrison and Bart gave the account giving the accent and mimicking Tony Morrison's squeaky voice.

"Right, phase one over. Tomorrow we start phase two. You had better make sure that those parts are all right before you send them to your customer, Bill?"

"I have and they are perfect. You see, he had a good training here. Pity it looks like it might be wasted."

The next day, Mr Tornton took a little run out to Upminster in his car. He stopped outside Upminster Laser and deliberately hung about before getting out of his car. He made sure that those inside saw he was there before going in. When he was sure that he had attracted the attention of those inside, he made his grand entrance.

"Hello, Mr Tebbs, or should I say Julian? The parts you

cut for me yesterday were excellent. I've come to give you another order."

"Oh, that's good," Julian answered all smiles. Standing with Julian were two other men.

"Are you going to introduce me to your colleagues?" asked old Mr Tornton acting as George Marshall.

"Er, yes," answered Julian. "This is Mr Morrison." The old man shook his hand. "And this is Mr Seals."

"How do you do?" said George Marshall.

Tony Morrison then took over. "I am Sales Director of this company and Robby here is our Quote Department Head."

"Then it's probably Robby I need to talk to." The old man then made it known that he was expecting a big order to come off in the very near future. Tony Morrison offered him a coffee and all three staff joined the old man in the accounts office.

"Yes, I was very impressed with the quality of the parts we received yesterday. We won't have to work much on them, only to paint them. Very good, yes, very good indeed."

"I'm pleased you were satisfied. What are they used for?" asked Tony Morrison. Of course the old man didn't know but bluffed his way through without batting an eyelid.

"They are used to support the production line at Ford Motor Company at Dagenham and Halewood," he answered quite matter of factly. "And over the next few months they are going to need thousands of them." He delved into his briefcase and produced another purchase order exactly the same as the last one. "I'm going to need another twenty by Wednesday, if you please. I don't suppose for one minute that you will have had answers back about our credit worthiness by then so, same as last time, I will see that cash is sent with the collection lorry."

Julian and Tony Morrison looked at each other and the old man realised that they were smiling to one another.

"Now, Mr Seals, how much is it going to cost me for two thousand of these parts exactly the same as you have already cut? I realise it's quite a big task but I will need them at the rate of five hundred a week?"

"If you give me a minute or two I'll work you out a price." Robby left the room but could be seen tapping away on a computer in the office next door through the frosted glass dividing panel. He could also be heard making telephone enquiries as to the price of material, emphasising the amount that was going to be needed.

Tony Morrison carried on with entertaining George Marshall. "Five hundred a week? That's quite a lot. We'll need to lay some transport on to move that amount."

"Don't worry about transport. If you can pack them in bundles of twenty and put two bundles on a pallet, we can get fourteen pallets on our large lorry, so it will be easier for us to collect. We've handled that quantity before. It makes the old lorry grunt a bit under the weight but we can manage that amount in one drop," answered the old man.

Robby returned and smiling, he said "I don't often get quotes as big as this," as he handed a copy of the quote to Tony Morrison and a copy to Mr Marshall.

The old man donned his glasses and read the document. "Yes," he said. "I take it that there is no delivery cost in this price, as we will be collecting ourselves?"

"No, Sir," answered Robby.

"Good, I think that's a very fair price. I've been quoted considerably higher than this. Eighty pounds is about what I had in mind. Good."

The old man then took his gold pen from his pocket and proceeded to write another forged purchase order out for twenty more conveyer supports, to be ready for collection in five days. He handed the document to Tony Morrison.

"There you are, my boy. We'll collect next Friday and, same as last time, I'll send the cash to save any hold ups. Mind you, our credit account should be open by then."

"Thank you. They'll be ready and I'll chase the paperwork to clear your credit account. I'm sure there will be no hitches," answered Tony Morrison. Tony walked with the old man to his car chatting about how tight business was and bid him farewell.

Ron wasn't completely aware of what Mr Tornton was up to. When he enquired, the old man just answered with a big smile, "Just like fishing. Set a sprat to catch a mackerel. Oh, and by the way, if any orders come through for Upminster Laser we can't supply. We are out of stock. I don't want them running up a bill with us that they can't pay."

"Right, I understand," replied Ron. He had a lot of respect for the old man and knew whatever he was up to, somebody was going to be very sorry.

Chapter 36

Bart was sent to collect the laser cut parts with the cash the same as last time. He made small conversation about how well his company was doing and that they were going to be working round the clock when they started installing a new production line at Ford's.

When he handed the money over to Julian he said, "The boss has asked me to ask if our account is open yet?"

Julian counted the money and answered, "I'll go and find out for you." Off he went to converse with Tony Morrison. They chatted for a minute or two. Bart could see them smiling to one another and, on his return, he said to Bart "Yes, your account is open but you are on strictly thirty days and we have agreed that your top limit is fifty thousand, in view of the fact you may have a big order in the pipeline."

"Good. I'll let the boss know."

"Tony Morrison is going to see your boss anyway, sometime this week, so he will put him in the picture."

"Oh, right."

Bart finished loading and as soon as he was out of sight of the laser firm he 'phoned his father to explain that Tony Morrison was thinking about visiting him. Bart was getting as excited as his dad at the prospect of these blokes digging their own graves.

"Don't worry, son, I'll sort it out," answered his dad. "You just take those parts you have just collected to

Precision Laser and leave the rest to me."

The old man telephoned Upminster Laser. "George Marshall here. Good morning, can I speak to Mr Morrison?"

"Morrison speaking. How are you, Mr Marshall? I was just talking about you. Your man's been to collect your order."

"Good. That's why I 'phoned, just to make sure that everything is all right. Did you receive payment?"

"We did, thank you. I was thinking of paying you a visit to outline your credit account and to see if there is any other work we can do for you?"

"That would be nice. When were you thinking of coming?"

"Maybe next week, sometime."

"Ah! I'm afraid I'm going to be at Halewood all next week. It's almost certain that the order I was telling you about is going to come off, so as soon as I know for sure I'll drop you a purchase order in the post so that you can get things moving. Oh, by the way, our credit rating, that you just mentioned, has it been cleared yet?"

"Yes. That was one of the things I wanted to discuss with you. We have put you on a thirty day account but if this big job comes off we couldn't afford to let your credit exceed fifty thousand."

"Of course you couldn't, my dear boy, and I wouldn't expect you to. I'll make some arrangement with you a little nearer the time. Look, I've given Julian my mobile phone number. If you need to reach me at any time, please call on that number. As I said, I will be at Halewood all next week and after that I will be at the Dagenham plant, so it's doubtful that you will catch me at the office at all over the next few weeks."

"O.K., Mr Marshall. Look forward to hearing from you. Let's hope the big job does come off, for both our sakes. Goodbye."

Mr Tornton put the phone down and laughed out loud. "They've fallen for it," he exclaimed. The first person he told was Bill Ross. Bill chuckled along with the old man.

"I hope they have after we've given them nearly four thousand pounds worth of work and paid up front for it," commented Bill.

"Yes, I know but it hasn't cost us anything, only a bit of time. You get your money back from your customer and if all goes according to plan you won't have to cut any more of those parts for ages. You'll be able to keep your customer supplied from the stock that they are going to give us free of charge."

"Hope you are right."

Ron had received an order from Upminster Laser for more extra large sheets of material and told them that on this occasion he couldn't help them as they were out of stock and that the next shipment wasn't due in for another six weeks.

Mr Tornton and Ron sat down and worked out a time schedule. They agreed that it would take about a week to cut five hundred parts providing that they worked a night shift.

"We'll give them eight days from Monday. That will give them enough time to get the material in and get it cut," said old man Tornton as he carefully wrote out the purchase order. The document asked for two thousand Conveyer Supports, part number 189732. The first batch of five hundred to be banded in batches of twenty, two batches on a pallet, and to be ready for collection on Tuesday the twenty first at a cost of eighty pounds per part plus VAT. The remaining fifteen hundred to be called off at the rate of five hundred a week unless otherwise notified.

He then put the document into an envelope and said, "I'll deliver this by hand, I think. I could do with a little run out for some fresh air." He smiled and kissed the envelope and drove off in his Daimler. Ron watched him drive away from the office window. Ron admired the smartly dressed elderly man more and more as he got to know him better. The old man was no fool and his mind was as sharp as a razor.

Friday afternoon arrived. Ron and Bill and old man Tornton were all together for the normal monthly meeting.

175

After discussing the items that were on the official agenda, Ron reminded the other two that Tuesday was collection day for Upminster Laser.

"Yes, we are well aware."

"Now you have bought the subject up, I had better give them a ring to see if every thing is going to plan," said Mr Tornton. The old man phoned and was assured that the first batch of five hundred would be ready on time. "Right, Ron, make sure that the large artic lorry is free on Tuesday and it might pay us to make sure that the Tornton name on the cab is covered up when we go for the collection."

"Right."

Bill Ross hadn't really thought that the old man was going to go through with it until now. All three sat and chuckled over the prospect of what was going to happen next Tuesday.

Over the weekend, Ron and Bill did manage to get a couple of games of snooker in at Bill's home. They were both amazed at the cunning of old man Tornton and the old man was the continual topic of conversation between the two of them.

Tuesday came. Bart went with the driver in the lorry to collect the consignment. Everything was ready for them. There were thirteen pallets in all and when they were loaded the weight showed on the lorry. It was well down on it's springs. Bart signed the delivery note and made enquiries about the next batch. Julian assured him that everything was in order and going according to plan.

The reception party was waiting at Precision Laser when the lorry arrived back. Old man Tornton, Bill Ross and Ron, all three were very excited at the prospect of getting one over on Tony Morrison and his crew at Upminster Laser. They were joined by Bart in Bill's office to get a full account of what was said and what had happened at the time of collection. Bart got a great deal of pleasure relaying step by step what had taken place and the fact that another load was going to be ready in a week's time. Porkie was unaware of what was going on. He had recognised the parts and at first thought that they had been returned faulty by Zenith Conveyers. He eventually got put in the picture by Ron. Not the full story because Ron really didn't know the whole story himself. Porkie was a bit jealous of Ron. He never understood how Ron could possibly manage Tornton Steels. Ron was aware of this and tried to treat him with the respect that a Production Manager was entitled to. Of course, Porkie knew Tony Morrison and Julian and he was delighted when he knew that Robby was involved as well.

The next day old John Tornton telephoned Upminster Laser and spoke to Tony Morrison.

"Morning, Marshall here. How are you?"

"Fine. Working hard to get your parts ready. We are having to work all night."

"That's the idea. Pleased you're busy, the parts we received yesterday were good. They have been painted and are on there way to Halewood. Thanks."

"The second batch will be ready on the twenty-eighth, next Tuesday but you do realise that will put you right over the credit limit we arranged?"

"Yes, of course, that's why I 'phoned. I'm way ahead of you. I have arranged for a Banker's draft for forty thousand to be raised in your favour and be given to you when we pick up the next load, if that's all right with you?"

"That's fine, Mr Marshall. Nice doing business with you. You will be able to pick them up first thing on Tuesday morning."

Over the next few days Mr Tornton made a couple of telephone calls to Tony Morrison just to make sure that things were going along all right and to reassure him that money was no problem. He told George Marshall that other customers were chasing him for their jobs because British Conveyers' job had occupied most of the machine time over the last week. He told him that he wouldn't mind jobs as big as this all the time. Mr Tornton, in his role of George Marshall, said, "Who knows, if this job goes according to plan then it may be repeated at the Dagenham plant and that would be an even bigger job."

"That would be nice," answered Tony Morrison. "We could do with another job like this one. It's nice to keep the machines running flat out," he remarked.

*   *   *

Tuesday the twenty eighth arrived. Bart and the driver set off early, as soon as the lorry arrived at Upminster Laser. Tony Morrison asked if Bart had got the cheque.

"No, the boss took it away from me, he did give it to me but he said he was going to 'phone you."

"Well, he hasn't"

"Phone him then. You can get him on his mobile. The number is…"

"Yeah, I've got the number. You can start loading but you're not leaving until I've got that bloody cheque." He went into the office, presumably to 'phone George Marshall.

"Hello."

"Is that you, Mr Marshall?"

"Yes, that you, Mr Morrison?"

"Yes. Your driver hasn't brought the cheque with him, as we agreed."

"I know. I was about to phone you. As I gave it to him this morning I suddenly realised that I had it drawn up and had omitted the VAT. I am on my way to you now with a draft for forty-seven thousand pounds and another one for the same amount dated the first of next month, which is in three days' time. I'm sure that will meet with your approval?" The phone went very quiet as Tony Morrison began to understand what he had just heard "Oh, yes, yes, of course, that's lovely," Tony Morrison answered, feeling pretty excited.

"Do me a favour, Mr Morrison. Get my lorry away as soon as you can. Those parts have to be painted and be in Halewood by tomorrow morning. I'll be with you by eleven o'clock. Get the kettle on and we'll have a coffee together."

"Right, will do. See you later."

Tony Morrison came out of the office with a smile on his face. He told Julian of the conversation he had just had and shouted, "Come on, get a move on. This lorry has got to get moving. It's got to be in Halewood by the morning."

As the lorry started up and slowly left the yard, Bart looked back in the rear view mirror and could see three men standing in the unit entrance watching the lorry move slowly away. They were Tony Morrison, Julian, and Robby.

The lorry was unloaded at Precision Laser and the contents were safely stacked away for future deliveries to Zenith Conveyers. Porkie commented that they wouldn't have to cut any of those parts now for years.

By mid-day Mr Tornton and Bill Ross were taking coffee in Bill's office. The old man's mobile phone rang several times. No-one answered it and every time it rang the two men looked at each other and smiled. "It's time I got rid of this," the old man said. "It doesn't belong to me, it belongs to the girlfriend of one of the lads from the plate shop at Tornton's. She lent it to me and now she has reported it stolen." Bill looked surprised. "Yes, I think it's time for this piece of technology to disappear. Can you smash it and dispose of it for me, Bill?" said the old man.

Bill agreed and made the necessary arrangements.

"You see, Bill, the only connection with us is the reference that we gave and I don't even suppose that they took any notice of that. All they could see was the cash from the first couple of orders." Bill felt a little uneasy but trusted the old man's judgement.

Chapter 37

Everything had gone very quiet. Bill was itching to find out what had happened at Upminster Laser when they found out that they had been conned. Mr Tornton carried on as though nothing had happened and took more and more time off, leaving the running of Tornton's to Ron aided by Bart. These two had indeed become quite friendly.

Ron was as curious as Bill and made several 'phone calls to other metal stockists in the area on the pretence of getting a credit reference for Upminster Laser. The answers he got were amazing. The biggest steel stockist was Armitage's. They told Ron, in no uncertain terms, that they wouldn't give Upminster Laser the time of day, let alone a credit reference and that if they didn't get a payment from them very soon that they were going to make them bankrupt. He got the same story from Brown Brothers and something very similar from South Essex Steels but they elaborated and said that the police were involved, because someone had conned them and taken them to the cleaners.

Ron got a lot of pleasure from telling Bill the story and although the excitement was over, both men felt they hadn't heard the last of it. Sure enough, the police called at Tornton's and made enquiries about the credit reference that was given for British Conveyers. Ron opened the files that referred to references and showed the police the reference had been given but for a firm called British Conveyers, of Streatham, South London and that if they had made a mistake they were extremely sorry and went on to say it was strange because no firm, especially one just starting up, gives anyone credit unless they have two or three company references and a solid reference from a bank. The police officers agreed and left, not entirely satisfied but, in the circumstances, prepared to give the benefit of the doubt to Tornton's.

Many weeks passed and it became common knowledge that Upminster Laser was in the hands of the Official Receivers and many stories were floating around the trade about how quickly a firm so young had got into trouble. The general consensus of opinion was that they must have been very inexperienced. Detective Sergeant Frost called on Bill at Precision Laser, under the pretence of it being a friendly visit as he was in the area. It was quite obvious that he was fishing for information about the bankruptcy at Upminster Laser to see if he could throw any light on what had happened.

"Yes, it is a shame. But how come you are on the case? It must be out of your area?" remarked Bill, feeling very slightly apprehensive.

"Oh it is. I'm not on the case but I've been asked to give you a call if I was in the area, by Romford CID. You see, it seems that Julian Tebbs thinks that you might have some involvement in what happened to them at Upminster. The people who pulled off this con gave your firm as a reference and, for obvious reasons, they didn't take the reference up with you."

"You are joking! I would not have given them a reference. I wouldn't even have answered anyway."

"I know but it is now obvious that the con men knew that as well."

"How does that involve me then?"

"It doesn't but at least I've done what I was asked to do. I've given you a call. You shouldn't hear any more about it."

As the Sergeant left to go he looked back at Bill and said, "These little crooks always get what's coming to them in the end, don't they?" and with a big grin on his face as he was closing the door said, "Well done!"